PENGUIN CLASSICS

RAJMOHAN'S WIFE

KIMCHANDRA CHATTOPADHYAY (1838–1894) was born
anthalpara, West Bengal. In 1858, he became the first Indian to
a BA degree. He served in the Indian Civil Service as Deputy
istrate and Deputy Collector between 1859 and 1891.

ohan's Wife was Bankimchandra's first novel, written in
sh. His first Bengali novel, *Durgeshnandini*, appeared in 1865.
vent on to write thirteen more novels, of which *Kapalkundala,*
alini, Bishabriksha, Krishnakanter Will, Rajani, Rajsingha and
i Choudhurani are the most famous. The epoch-making
ndamath appeared in 1882; the verse 'Vande Mataram' from the
el became the anthem of nationalists during the freedom movement,
is now the national song of India.

art from his novels, Bankimchandra has to his credit a considerable
dy of non-fiction. He was the editor of *Bangadarshan*, perhaps
e most influential literary magazine of its time, which began
ublication in 1872.

Rajmohan's Wife

BANKIMCHANDRA CHATTOPADHYAY

With an Introduction, Notes and
Afterword by

MEENAKSHI MUKHERJEE

RAVI DAYAL Publisher

PENGUIN BOOKS

PENGUIN BOOKS

Published by the Penguin Group

Penguin Books India Pvt. Ltd, 11 Community Centre, Panchsheel Park,
New Delhi 110 017, India

Penguin Group (USA) Inc., 375 Hudson Street, New York, New York 10014,
USA

Penguin Group (Canada), 90 Eglinton Avenue East, Suite 700, Toronto,
Ontario, M4P 2Y3, Canada (a division of Pearson Penguin Canada Inc.)

Penguin Books Ltd, 80 Strand, London WC2R 0RL, England

Penguin Ireland, 25 St Stephen's Green, Dublin 2, Ireland (a division of
Penguin Books Ltd)

Penguin Group (Australia), 250 Camberwell Road, Camberwell,
Victoria 3124, Australia (a division of Pearson Australia Group Pty Ltd)

Penguin Group (NZ), 67 Apollo Drive, Rosedale, North Shore 0632,
New Zealand (a division of Pearson New Zealand Ltd)

Penguin Group (South Africa) (Pty) Ltd, 24 Sturdee Avenue, Rosebank,
Johannesburg 2196, South Africa

Penguin Books Ltd, Registered Offices: 80 Strand, London WC2R 0RL, England

First published by Ravi Dayal Publisher 1996

Published by Ravi Dayal Publisher and Penguin Books India 2009

This edition copyright © Penguin Books India 2009
Introduction, Notes and Afterword copyright © Meenakshi Mukherjee 1996, 2009

All rights reserved

10 9 8 7 6 5 4 3 2 1

ISBN 9780143067436

Typeset in Perpetua by Gurutypograph Technology, Delhi
Printed at Pauls Press, New Delhi

CONTENTS

Introduction	vii
Preface	xii
The Drawers of Water	1
The Two Cousins	7
The Truant's Return Home	11
The History of the Rise and Progress of a Zemindar Family	14
A Letter—a Visit to the Zenana	23
Midnight Plotting	29
Love Can Conquer Fear	37
Forewarned and Forearmed	45
We Meet to Part	53
The Return	58
When Thieves Fall Out	63
The Friends and the Stranger	69
The Protectress	74
Between Rival Charmers	80
Consultations and Council	89

Contents

What Befell Our Hero   95

The Vigilance of Love   99

Captors and Captive   104

Madhav and Tara   113

Some Women Are the Equals of Some Men   119

The Last Chapter in Life's Book—and In This   123

Conclusion   127

Afterword   128

Notes   146

Introduction

SOMETIME IN 1864, A TWENTY-SIX-YEAR-OLD DEPUTY MAGISTRATE posted in Khulna district (Bengal Presidency) wrote a novel in English called *Rajmohan's Wife*. It was serialized in a short-lived weekly magazine published from Calcutta, but did not appear as a book in the author's lifetime. As the first Indian novel in English, *Rajmohan's Wife* has for well over a century been a text more heard of than read. The present edition is an attempt to make this unusual but neglected novel available to the general reader who may read it for the mere pleasure of the narrative and also, hopefully, to enable the specialized reader of literature situate it in the genealogy of the novel, a genre shaped in India by the contending pulls of colonial education and indigenous traditions of storytelling.

This early fictional work of Bankimchandra Chatterjee/Chattopadhyay (1838–94) subsequently got overshadowed by the fourteen novels he wrote in Bangla—*Durgeshnandini* (1865), *Anandamath* (1882) and *Rajsingha* (1893) among them—which were widely read, emulated, discussed and translated into many other Indian languages. *Rajmohan's Wife* never had that kind of visibility, partly because the book was not easily accessible, but also because most commentators and critics of Bankimchandra have regarded his foray into English writing as 'a false start' after which he is supposed to have found his true metier in Bangla.

Read today, after one hundred and forty-six years of its first appearance, *Rajmohan's Wife* remains a fascinating text for a number of reasons. In India, the novel as a genre was in its infancy in 1864 and, while romance was acceptable as a narrative mode, there was no precedent as yet of mimetic rendering of domestic life in fiction, or of weaving a plot out of contemporary social and familial situations. Yet *Rajmohan's Wife* is very nearly realistic in its representation of East Bengal middle-class life. The story of the beautiful and passionate Matangini married to a villainous man is astonishingly rich in vivid details in the description of interiors and the quotidian routine of women's lives. It goes beyond realism in the evocative use of nature—as, for example, in the description of Matangini's secret journey through a dark and stormy night, which uses the descriptive conventions of Vaishnava love poetry, and in anticipating several of Bankimchandra's more mature novels where landscape and nature are employed as narrative motifs.

There is also an attempt in *Rajmohan's Wife* to foreground the ways in which the home and the world are inextricably linked—a connection which happened to be of some concern to the classic realist novelists of nineteenth-century Europe also—by locating the drama within the conjugal and domestic space in relation to the external arena of property, legality, crime and the colonial administration. Inscribed in the text we also find an early statement about the helplessness and claustrophobia of women in incompatible marriages that was going to be a recurrent concern of Indian fiction for many years to come. Given the rigidness of the power structure within the family among upper-caste Bengalis in the nineteenth century, it seems surprising that the first Indian novel in a contemporary setting should have focused on a woman of uncommon vitality who refused to be completely subjugated either by her brutal husband or by the expectations of society. Matangini's unrequited love for her own sister's husband is presented with authorial sympathy, but the abruptness and the ambivalence of the ending may be the result of an anxiety such women of energy generated, by posing a threat to the social order and creating a moral dilemma for the author.

The other aspect of the novel that specially intrigues us today is the language. Now, in the first decade of the twenty-first century, when many more Indians are writing in English than ever before, we are so accustomed to this literary phenomenon that we seldom pause to reflect on why, and for which audience, a Bengali or a Marathi or a Tamil writer should want to write in English. When Bankimchandra, who was in the first graduating batch of the newly founded Calcutta University, began to write *Rajmohan's Wife*, he must have known that the English-reading population of Bengal was not very widespread. Did he visualize very clearly who was going to be his reader? The half-hearted attempts at textual explanations of cultural details indicate a vague awareness of readers who may be outsiders to the Bengali way of life—possibly the British administrators in India—but given the historical circumstances and the place of publication, this could not have comprised a sizeable readership. His subsequent decision of never again writing fiction in English may have had as much to do with his realization of the illusory nature of his audience as with his nationalist ideology, or his honest artistic self-appraisal. In *Rajmohan's Wife* Bankimchandra's attempt to negotiate the semantic and connotative hurdles that are involved in rendering an Indian (in this case Bengali) ethos in the English language, without any previous model whatsoever, forces us to think about the interconnectedness of culture and language, narrative voice and implied readership—issues that have not ceased to be relevant. It also makes us go beyond literary questions about how well one writes in English to non-literary enquiries regarding the publication, distribution and marketing of a literary product in the local, national or global market. It is indeed worth considering the complex circumstances that made Bankimchandra shift from English to the mother tongue before he could gain national recognition, while in early twenty-first-century India one would expect the process to be reversed.

The present text is reprinted from the 1935 version edited by Brajendra Nath Banerji, whose Preface is also included here. The history of the text is as follows. It was first serialized in *Indian Field*, a small-circulation journal edited by Kishori Chand Mitra, who, like Bankimchandra, had been in the Bengal Civil Service, but for reasons I have not been able to trace, lost his job in 1858. Issues of this weekly were not easily available even in 1935, and are certainly not available now. When Brajendra Nath Banerji located all but the first three chapters (see the Preface by Banerji), these missing chapters were retranslated (probably by Banerji) from a Bengali translation of the English novel that Bankimchandra himself had begun. This reconstructed whole was published in *The Modern Review* (1935) and also appeared as a book in the same year from Calcutta. Subsequently, it was included in Volume III of the collected works of Bankimchandra Chattopadhyay (*Bankim Rachanabali*) edited by Jogesh Chandra Bagal and published by the Bangiya Sahitya Samsad in 1969. The footnotes from these earlier editions have been omitted in the present edition. These annotations were somewhat arbitrary and casual, because, while some Bangla words were explained, others were left untouched. The Notes in the present edition are provided by me and not all of them are explicatory. They also seek to comment on the text and speculate on authorial intention. The critical essay at the end of the volume ('Afterword') raises questions that are both textual and cultural, and is aimed at those who would like to place *Rajmohan's Wife* in a literary/historical perspective. I am thankful to two friends—Rajeshwari Sunder Rajan and Harish Trivedi, whose opinion I value—for having gone through an earlier draft of the essay patiently and making detailed suggestions. If the Afterword still remains fragmentary and tentative, I accept the blame for that.

MEENAKSHI MUKHERJEE

Preface

STRANGELY ENOUGH, BENGAL'S FIRST GREAT NOVELIST, LIKE Bengal's first great modern poet, made his debut in the field of literature in the English language. Bankimchandra Chattopadhyay was only twenty-seven when he won a permanent place in the history of Bengali literature with his first novel in his mother tongue, *Durgeshnandini*, published in 1865. Two years before that he had completed a novel in English. This was entitled *Rajmohan's Wife* and was published as a serial in 1864 in the weekly periodical, the *Indian Field*, edited by Kishori Chand Mitra. The files of the *Indian Field* being now almost unobtainable, the existence of a complete English novel by Bankimchandra Chattopadhyay was almost forgotten, and even his biographer and nephew, Mr Sachis Chandra Chatterjee, has stated that Bankim did not finish this English novel. A happy chance has, however, enabled me to recover the complete story with the exception of the first three chapters. I had occasion, in connection with a different line of investigation, to go through the files of the famous Anglo-Bengali paper *Hindoo Patriot* for 1864, facilities for consulting which were very kindly obtained for me by Sir Jadunath Sarkar from Mr Sitanath Pal, a grandson of the great Bengali publicist, Kristodas Pal. With this volume of the *Hindoo Patriot* was found bound by chance all but three of the issues of the *Indian Field* in which Bankim's novel had appeared. Thus the historian of Bengali literature has reason to be grateful for a binder's mistake.

This first serious work of Bankimchandra Chattopadhyay
is now made accessible to a wider circle of readers than could
possibly consult the files of the long-defunct *Indian Field*. As
regards the missing first three chapters of Bankim's original,
it has been possible to substitute for them a version as close
to Bankim's own as could be desired. At a later period of his
life Bankim himself had begun to prepare a Bengali version of
his first novel. But he did not proceed further than the first
seven chapters of the English original. This fragment was
completed in his own way by his nephew, Mr Sachis Chandra
Chatterjee, who did not know that the fragment was actually
a Bengali rendering of the English original, *Rajmohan's Wife*.
He, on the contrary, believed it to be an entirely new work
and gave to the joint production the name of *Vari-Vahini*. It is
by means of a translation of the first three chapters of this
Bengali book that the missing beginning of Bankim's English
novel has been here supplied. *Rajmohan's Wife*, as published
by us now, thus comprises Bankim's own original English from
Chapter IV to the 'Conclusion', and our English rendering of
Bankim's Bengali version from Chapters I to III.

1935   BRAJENDRA NATH BANERJI

The Drawers of Water[1]

THERE IS A SMALL VILLAGE ON THE RIVER MADHUMATI. ON ACCOUNT of its being the residence of wealthy zemindars it is regarded as a village of importance. One Chaitra[2] afternoon the summer heat was gradually abating with the weakening of the once keen rays of the sun; a gentle breeze was blowing; it began to dry the perspiring brow of the peasant in the field and play with the moist locks of village women just risen from their siesta.

It was after such a siesta that a woman of about thirty was engaged in her toilet in a humble thatched cottage. She took very little time to finish the process usually so elaborate with womankind; a dish of water, a tin-framed looking-glass three inches wide, and a comb matching it sufficed for the task. Then, a little vermilion adorned her forehead. Last of all some betel leaves dyed her lips. Thus armed, a formidable champion of the world-conquering sex set out with a pitcher in her arm and pushing open the wattled gate of a neighbouring house entered within it.

There were four huts in the house which she entered. They had mud floors and bamboo walls. There was no sign of poverty anywhere, everything was neat and tidy. The four huts stood on the four sides of a quadrangle. Of these three had entrances opening on the yard, the fourth opened outwards. This last was the reception room, while the others, screened on all sides, constituted the zenana.[3] Some brinjals and salads[4] were growing on the carefully tilled plot of land in front of the raised terrace before the outer room. The whole was enclosed by a reed fence with a bamboo gate. So the woman could easily make her way into the house.

It is superfluous to add that she went straight towards the zenana. I know not where the other inmates of the house had gone after their siesta, but at that time there were only two persons there—one, a young woman of eighteen bent over her embroidery and a child of four immersed in play. His elder brother had wilfully left his inkpot behind when going to school. The child's eyes had fallen on it, and he was joyfully smearing his face with the ink. He seemed to be afraid of his brother coming back and snatching the inkpot away, and so was emptying the pot. The newcomer sat down on the floor by the side of her who was working and asked, 'What are you doing?'

The other laughed and said, 'Oh, it's Didi. What kindness! Whose face was it that I first saw on getting up this morning?'

The guest laughed back and retorted, 'Who else but the person you see every morning?'

At this, the face of the younger woman clouded over for a moment, while the smile half lingered on the lips of the other. Let us describe them both at this place.[5]

It has already been mentioned that the visitor was thirty years of age. She was neither dark nor exactly olive; her face was not quite pretty, yet there was no feature which displeased the eye; she had a sort of restless charm, and her smiling eyes heightened the effect of it. The ornaments on her person were not large in number, but constituted a fair load for a porter. The conch-shell worker who had made her shell bracelet was no doubt a descendant of Visvakarma himself. The woman adorned with these ornaments had only a coarse sari on her plump figure. There was evidently no love lost between the sari and the washerman, for it had not visited the laundry for a long time.

The dainty limbs of the woman of eighteen were not burdened with such abundance of ornaments, nor did her speech betray any trace of the East Bengal accent, which clearly showed that this perfect flower of beauty was no daughter of the banks of the Madhumati, but was born and brought up on the Bhagirathi[6] in some place near the capital. Some sorrow or deep anxiety had dimmed the lustre of her fair complexion. Yet her bloom was as full of charm as that of the land-lotus half scorched and half radiant under the noonday sun. Her long locks were tied up in a careless knot on her shoulder; but some loose tresses had thrown away that bondage and were straying over her forehead and cheeks. Her faultlessly drawn arched eyebrows were quivering with bashfulness under a full and wide forehead. The eyes were often only half seen under their drooping lids. But when they were raised for a glance, lightning seemed to play in a summer cloud. Yet even those keen glances charged with the fire of youth betrayed anxiety. The small lips indicated the sorrow nursed in her heart. The beauty of her figure and limbs had been greatly spoilt by her physical or mental suffering. Yet no sculptor had ever created anything nearly as perfect as the form half revealed by the neat sari she wore. The well-shaped limbs were almost entirely bare of ornaments. There were only *churis* on the wrists and a small amulet on her arm. These too were elegant in shape.

The younger woman put away her needlework and began to talk with the visitor. The latter displayed great eloquence in describing her domestic tribulations, most of which unfortunately were imaginary. She put the fringe of her mud-stained sari again and again to her eyes, which were not in a condition to call for it. But in certain eventualities even the *Salagram*[7] (god) dies. As often as the end of the sari touched her eyes, they shed copious tears. After many such showers she was preparing for a full-dress outburst when her eyes suddenly fell on the ink-smeared face of the child who had emptied the inkpot and was standing with a darkened countenance. The bizarre sight converted the tears of the narrator of household misery into laughter; humour swept away pathos.

When the ceremony of tears ended at last, the sun was really sinking down to rest. At this the speaker invited the young woman to come with her to fetch water. She had in fact come there with a view to making that invitation. The younger woman refused, and when her companion began to press her, said, 'There are crocodiles in the Madhumati. They will drag me away.'

Her companion laughed out loudly at this, which showed her that her objection was not admitted. Yet she added, 'You should go now, Kanak. It's growing late.'

Kanak pointed to the sun which was still above the trees and said, 'It's still noon.'

At this the younger woman became grave and said, 'You know, Kanak Didi, I never fetch water.'

'That is why I am asking you to,' replied Kanak. 'Why should you remain in a cage all the day. Do not all other housewives draw water?'

The younger woman said disdainfully, 'That's a work for servant-girls.'

'Why, who fetches water for you? Where are your servants?'

'Well, Thakurjhi[8] fetches our water.'

'If the daughter can do servants' work, cannot the daughter-in-law?'

The young woman said firmly, 'I cannot argue about it, Kanak. You know my husband has forbidden me to fetch water, and you know him well.'

Kanakmayee did not reply offhand. She quickly glanced round to see if anyone was coming. When she saw there was no one about, she stood with her eyes fixed on the face of her companion as if wanting to say something. But she repressed the impulse from fear and remained musing with downcast eyes. The younger girl asked, 'What are you thinking about?'

'If only you had eyes,' replied Kanak.

The younger woman would not, however, listen to her. She made a sign to Kanak to stop and said, 'Hush, hush, I understand your meaning.'

'If you have done so, what are you going to do now?' asked Kanak.

The younger girl remained silent for a while. Her quivering lips and reddening brow betrayed the preoccupation of her mind. A slight tremor in her limbs also showed how agitated she was. After some time she said, 'Let us go, but is it wrong?'

Kanak laughed and replied, 'Wrong! I am not a fat-bellied Bhattacharya. I have nothing to do with the Shastras. But I would have gone even if I had fifty men.'

'Oh! What bravery!' replied the other laughing as she went out to get her pitcher. 'Fifty! Do you really wish for as many?'

Kanak smiled sadly and said, 'It's a sin even to say so. But if all the fifty were of the same sort as the one given me by Fate, it would hardly matter. If I meet none, I am a chaste and devoted wife even if married to a crore of men.'

'The Kulin girl's[9] lot!' exclaimed the other and quickly got a tiny pitcher from the kitchen. The pitcher perfectly matched the carrier of water. Then they both marched off towards the river. Kanak laughed and said, 'Come now, my proud girl, let's go and show beauty's splendour to the gaping idiots.'

'Hang you, monkey!'[10] cried the other and hid her blushing face in her veil.

The Two Cousins

THE RAYS OF THE SETTING SUN HAD VANISHED FROM THE TOPS OF the cocoanut palms. But night had not yet descended on the earth. It was at this time that Kanak and her companion were returning home, each with a pitcher in her arm. By the roadside was a small garden, of a type rare in East Bengal.[1] Numerous roses and *mallika* buds were caressing the eyes of the passers-by from within the compound surrounded by a handsome iron fence. Walks covered with red brick-dust had been laid down beside the old-style square and oval beds. There was a tank in the middle of the garden, whose banks were covered with soft turf. On one side was a row of brick-paved steps. Facing the steps was the reception room, in the front veranda of which two men were engaged in talk.

The older of the two would be above thirty. He was a tall and stout man. It was because he was too stout that he could not be said to possess a good figure. His complexion was dull and dark. There was no feature on his face which could give him the least claim to handsomeness. On the contrary he had something positively unattractive about him. In fact, his was not a common face; at the same time it was difficult to define its peculiarity offhand. He had a dhoti of Dacca manufacture on.[2] A long and twisted Dacca chudder was tied round his head in the shape of a turban which hid even the few wisps of hair that still remained there. His dark and corpulent body could be fully seen through the shirt of Dacca muslin he was wearing, and with it his gold amulet which peeped out off and on. But the thick gold chain which adorned his neck had actually intruded outside his shirt. The shirt had gold studs fastened with a gold chain; all the fingers had rings; and there was a huge bludgeon of peach in his hand. The two small feet were enclosed in English shoes.

This man's companion was a remarkably handsome young man of about twenty-two. His clear placid complexion had turned a little dull either through want of exercise or too much comfort. His clothes were good but not very costly; a dhoti, a fine chudder, a cambric shirt and English shoes. There was a single ring on one finger, and no amulet or necklace. The elder man addressed the other, 'Well Madhav, you have turned to Calcutta again. Why this infatuation?'

'Infatuation?' replied Madhav. 'If my liking for Calcutta be an infatuation, why shouldn't yours for Radhaganj be called by the same name?'

Mathur asked, 'Why?'

Madhav. 'Why not? You have spent your life in the shade of the mango gardens of Radhaganj. You love Radhaganj. I have spent my life in the stench of Calcutta. I love Calcutta.'

Mathur. 'Stench only? The filth of the drains with rotten rats and cats thrown in. Surely a feast for the gods!'

Madhav smiled and said, 'It is not for these that I go to Calcutta. I have business, too.'

Mathur: 'Business indeed! New horses, new carriages, visiting all the sharks of the town, throwing away money, burning the oil, drinks for anglicized friends, and pleasures. What are you staring at that way? Have you never seen Kanak? Or has the girl with her just dropped from the sky? Ah, yes! Who is it with her?'

Madhav flushed, but immediately changed the subject and said, 'What a girl Kanak is! She can laugh with so much sorrow eating into her heart.'

Mathur: 'Yes. But who is it she's got with her.'

Madhav: 'How can I say? I cannot see through clothes. You see she is veiled.'

It was in fact Kanak and her companion who were returning with their pitchers. Everybody knew Kanak. But such indescribable beauty radiated from every movement of the other woman that it charmed the eyes first of Madhav and then of Mathur. Their looks remained fixed on her and they were as fascinated by the sight as a deer is by the sound of the flute.

When the words last recorded came out of the mouth of Madhav, a sudden gust of wind passed over the heads of the women. The younger woman was then adjusting the pitcher in arms still unused to carrying water, and she had brought down her hand from the veil. The wind blew it away and revealed the face. Madhav raised his brows in surprise. Mathur said, 'There, you know her.'

'Yes.'

'You know her and I do not? I have spent my life here and you are only a newcomer. Well, if you know her, who is she?'

'My sister-in-law.'

'Your sister-in-law? Rajmohan's wife!'

'Yes.'

'Rajmohan's wife, and I have not seen her!'

'How can you? She never leaves her house.'

'Why then has she today?'

'I don't know.'

'What sort of a woman is she?'

'You have seen her.——Very handsome.'

'Oh, a thought-reader indeed! I am not asking that. Is she a good woman?'

'What do you mean by a "good woman"?'

Mathur: 'Oh, what the college has done for you! It's impossible to talk with people who have once gone there and recited the jargon of the red-faced sahibs. What I mean is—has she—'

The stern frown of Madhav cut short the coarse speech forming on Mathur's lips.

Madhav said haughtily, 'You need not be so outspoken. You have no business to prattle about a respectable woman passing along the road.'

Mathur replied, 'Did I not say that a smattering of English converts our brethren into fiery sahibs! Well, if one is not to discuss one's sister-in-law, whom is one to discuss—his grandmother? Anyway, let it pass. Relax your scowling face, or the crows would begin to peck at it. What luck! That clown Rajmohan to have a wife like this!'

'Marriage is called a lottery,' said Madhav.

And after a few more words the two parted company.

The Truant's Return Home

KANAKMAYEE AND HER COMPANION SILENTLY PURSUED THEIR WAY home. The latter was feeling extremely shy before men, and at her silence Kanak also had to remain silent. Kanak, however, felt the missed opportunity of wagging her tongue very keenly. The pathway was more lonely near their homes, and the younger woman began, 'How the wretched wind hustled me!'

'Why?' replied Kanak laughingly. 'Has your brother-in-law never seen you before?'

'I am not thinking of him. But there was another man with him.'

'He is Mathur Babu. Have you never seen him?'

'No, indeed! Is he Mathur Babu, the cousin of my sister's husband?'

'Yes, who else?'

'What a shame! Please don't talk about it to anybody.'

'Oh no! I am going to tell people that you dropped your veil and showed your face when coming back from the river,' said Kanak, and began to simper. The younger woman said angrily, 'Go to Jericho![1] How she goes on! I would never have come with you if I had known—'

Kanak laughed again.

'Leave your jokes alone.—O horror! Durga save me!' cried out the young woman as she cast her eyes towards her house and began to tremble. They were at that time quite close to it. Kanak saw Rajmohan standing at the door with glaring eyes, the very image of Death, and whispered to her companion, 'There is trouble for you! Let me go in with you. I might be of some help.'

Rajmohan's wife replied in the same low tone, 'Oh no! I am quite used to it. It would probably be worse if you are there. You had better go home.'

At this Kanak went her way. Rajmohan did not speak to his wife when she entered the house. She went to the kitchen to put her pitcher down. He followed her silently there. When she had set it down, he said to her, 'Wait a moment,' and poured out all the water on the dustheap. Rajmohan had an old aunt who used to do his cooking. She scolded Rajmohan for thus wasting the water. 'Why are you throwing the water away? You don't keep a score of servants to draw water.'

'Shut up, you old hag,' cried out Rajmohan and flung away the empty pitcher. The he turned round to his wife and said in a softer but scathing tone. 'Well, queen, where have you been?' The woman firmly whispered back, 'I had gone to fetch water.' She was standing like a statue exactly on the spot where her husband had asked her to stop.

'To fetch water!' taunted Rajmohan. 'But with whose permission did you go out?'

'With nobody's permission.'

Rajmohan could restrain himself no longer. 'With nobody's permission!' he shouted. 'Have I not forbidden you a thousand times?'

The woman replied in the same even tone, 'You have.'

'Then, wretched girl, why did you go?'

The woman proudly replied, 'I am your wife.' Her face reddened and her voice began to be choked. 'I had gone because I thought there was nothing wrong in it.'

At this display of boldness, Rajmohan absolutely blazed up. 'Have I not forbidden you a thousand times?' he shouted, and jumping on his wife who was standing stock-still, gripped her by the wrist, raising his other hand to strike her.

The helpless woman seemed to understand nothing. She did not move away one step from her assailant, but only looked at him with such pathetic eyes that his hand remained motionless as if spellbound. After a moment's silence Rajmohan dropped his wife's hand, but immediately shouted out, 'I'll kick you to death.'

Even then the chidden woman did not reply. Only tears were streaming down her face. At the sight of her silent suffering the cruel man softened a little. He no longer tried to beat her, but continued his abuse. It is unnecessary to try the patience of my readers by reproducing all of his Billingsgate.[2] The patient woman bore it silently. When, at last, Rajmohan's anger ebbed away, his aunt gathered some courage. She took her nephew's wife by the hand and led her into a room, all the while scolding her nephew. Even that was done circumspectly. But when she saw at last that Rajmohan had almost cooled down she burst out in her turn and paid the nephew back in his own coin. Rajmohan was then nursing his own grievances. He could not quite appreciate the language of his aunt. At any rate there was no novelty in it, for he had heard it many times before. So they both parted. The aunt began to console the wife, and Rajmohan went out pondering whom to fall upon and smash up.

The History of the
Rise and Progress of a
Zemindar Family

IT IS A NOTORIOUS FACT THAT MANY EMINENT ZEMINDAR FAMILIES in Bengal owe their rise to some ignoble origin.

Bangshibadan Ghose lived as a menial servant with an old zemindar of East Bengal whose name and family are now extinct. The unfruitfulness of his first marriage induced the zemindar, late in life, to take another wife, but it had been preordained that he should live and die childless. He had, however, a blessing which next to a progeny he deemed the greatest good that could befall him in his old age—a young and beautiful wife. It is true indeed that discordance and broils between his two helpmates often interrupted his domestic felicity, for the elder lady always sturdily maintained that seniority constituted the indisputable rule by which favours should be bestowed, which indisputable rule, however, the old gentleman always presumed to dispute. Matters were getting to a hopeless state when interfered an umpire whose award brooked no question, and justly acknowledging the claims of her own indefeasible right of seniority removed the elder lady to another world. The old man and his youthful mate were now left in peace, but the former justly took warning by the occurrence and perceived that he himself might be called upon to follow at no distant day. Now hopeless of leaving a family, he reflected with bitterness that his ample estates must be left to the enjoyment of those who had been to him almost strangers, and that though they might remain in the possession of his wife during her lifetime, she could not, with her hands fettered by a law,[1] be anything more than a pensioner on her own estate. Desirous of leaving it in a condition which should leave the young woman its complete mistress, and led into the same course by the advice and influence of his wife, whose perception of her own future prospects was wonderfully clear, he began to free his possessions of landed incumbrances and to convert his zemindaris into ready money and movables as often as he could advantageously do it, and so successful was his uxorious zeal that when he died his relict[2] became the mistress of a splendid fortune of which landed property formed a very inconsiderable portion. Now Karunamayee was a decidedly sensible woman, and she judged it right that, mistress of her fortune and her person, she should enjoy both. Ram, the godhead, she argued, had, in the depth of his love and gratitude for his adored wife, consoled himself in the days of his bereavement by a metallic representative of Sita. Why then should not her immense love for her departed husband find expression under the same representative system? She also thought that it would be a decided improvement in the plan, if she made a human being instead of a metallic image represent the loved and lost one for whom she mourned, inasmuch as a human being is a nobler thing, and would bear a closer resemblance than metal, and also as such resemblance would by no means be confined to the external form alone. Thus fortified by reason and veneration for the departed as well as by the example of the gods, she lost no time in making her choice. Bangshibadan Ghose the menial servant was the happy mortal on whom it fell. This crafty person

perceived his advantage too clearly to neglect it, and lord of
his mistress's bosom, he saw no reason [why][3] he should nor
be the same of her fortune. It was an easy achievement and
his progress from the rank of Khansama to that of Sadar Naib[4]
was rapid. A fever originally slight, but which from unintelligible
or rather very intelligible causes, became fearfully violent, forced
the anxious widow to part with her domestic and with the world
before age had chilled her fires. A few days after, the distant
and expectant relatives of her husband came to take possession
of her estates, but found to their great mortification that they
consisted only of a few wretched villages. Of movables, they
were told, there were only a few and these she had given
away to her servants.

Bangshibadan carried with him a splendid fortune to
Radhaganj, the seat of his humble paternal abode. He very
prudently made no display of his immense wealth, except so
much as was necessary to a life of comfort. On his demise
he left a splendid patrimony to each of his three sons. These,
who deemed long possession had conferred security, were no
longer restrained by the same prudential considerations as
their father, purchased zemindaris, built fine houses, and
assumed the state and style that belonged to their wealth. The
eldest Ramkanta by dint of prudent and able management
improved his share, and after having lived to a green old age[5]
bequeathed it to the equally able or abler hands of his only
son, Mathur, with whom we have had the pleasure of making
the reader acquainted. Ramkanta had viewed with eyes of
jealousy the encroachments that were being made in the
ancient manners and usages by the influence of Western
civilization and had steadily forborne to send his son to an
English school, which he condemned as a thing not only useless

but as positively mischievous. Mathur was early associated with his father in the management of the zemindari and proved an exceedingly apt scholar in the science of chicane, fraud and torture.

The fate of Ramkanai, the second son of Bangshibadan, was different. By nature indolent and extravagant, he soon managed to throw his affairs into disorder. His houses and gardens were the most magnificent, his estates the most unprofitable and the worst managed. Some wily hangers-on, too, played on his credulity and painted to him in alluring colours the chances which a certain mercantile scheme they propounded presented of retrieving his affairs. Ramkanai followed their advice and, placing himself under their guidance, took up his residence in Calcutta. It is needless to add that his advisers continued to fleece him of every farthing he had ventured in the speculation and eventually to bring his mismanaged and neglected estates to the hammer.

One good result, however, had followed Ramkanai's residence in the metropolis. Influenced by the example of the metropolitans, he had bestowed on his son Madhav as good an education as he could receive in Calcutta. He had also accomplished that great object of a Hindu father's love—the marriage of his son with a girl of remarkable beauty. A poor Kayastha dwelt in a small village in the vicinity of Calcutta, who boasted that the only good fortune that the heavens had conferred on him was perfect in its kind, and his two daughters had not their equal in beauty or in dutiful and amiable conduct. But the same circumstances which often so cruelly match the fairest and tenderest of fair and tender Bengalis, consigned the eldest of his daughters, the noble and beautiful Matangini, to the arms of the brutal Rajmohan; yet, when the marriage

took place, Matangini's father thought he had not chosen
ill. Rajmohan had indeed then reached manhood and was
therefore unsuited in age—but this was not minded much. He
possessed no handsome person—but a handsome person was
to be looked for in a boy bridegroom, not in a man. He lived
in an adjoining village, and the prospect that no great distance
would separate father and daughter served greatly to favour
the match in the eyes of the former. His robust frame and
vast strength were the envy and admiration of all who knew
him. His spirit was active and energetic, ready in expedients,
and as a natural consequence, though his father had left him
no fortune and given him no education, he was never much in
want. This circumstance which promised to rescue Matangini
from the pinchings of poverty seemed to her father to be
another and the greatest recommendation, and the marriage
accordingly took place. The younger and more fortunate
Hemangini became the bride of young Madhav.

The father of Madhav died a little before the latter
completed his studies at college. He would have been left
penniless but for a circumstance which nobody had foreseen.

Ramgopal the third son of Bangshibadan was neither so
fortunate as the first, nor so unfortunate as the second.
He died early and childless bequeathing nearly the whole of
his property to his nephew Madhav on condition the latter
maintained his relict as long as she lived in Madhav's household.

Madhav continued his studies till he finished them, his
agents managing his estate for him during his absence and
minority. After the expiration of the year, he prepared to leave
the city for Radhaganj with his young and beautiful wife. Before
[going there he] took her to her father's house in order [to
enable her to] bid her parents farewell. [Madhav's wife] was

beloved by her sister, [and design] or accident brought also Rajmohan [and his wife to the] house.

Madhav intended to make a short stay with his father-in-law; Hemangini incessantly wept at the prospect of parting with her parents and her sister, for how long she knew not. It was a far, far country whither she was going, and would she ever come back to the scene of her earliest affection? Would her parents ever visit her there? Her father said he would, but then her mother? Her sister? Her mother and sister answered not, but wept with her in silence, and gave her their blessings.

Matangini took hold of her sister's hand and drew her aside. When they were alone, she said, 'Hem, I have something to ask of you.' Hemangini did not reply but gazed upon her sister with an enquiring look in her large black eyes.

'Hem,' Matangini resumed, 'we part tomorrow.'

Hemangini burst into tears. 'Weep not, sister,' said Matangini, calming her own agitated features with effort, 'weep not; the gods will bless you, and you have a husband, Hem, who will make you happy.' As she said this, warm tears ran down her cheeks and fell upon the lily hands that she held in her own.

'What were you going to ask of me?' enquired Hemangini, wiping her eyes.

'I am poor, Hem, very poor, but were it for me only I would never speak of it to you. But my husband, whatever he is, sister, Heaven made him so—he is my husband and I care for him. He has now nothing to do and is reduced to great straits. He has besought me to ask you to speak to my brother-in-law.'

'Yes, I will; but what shall I ask in his behalf?'

'An employment—some means of earning a livelihood.'

'I will,' promised Hem, and then the sisters conversed on other subjects.

Hemangini had in the ardour of her affection for her sister undertaken a task which she knew not how to execute. She was still of that tender age when wives in her country[6] speak always timidly to their husbands, and hardly ever on such subjects. She mustered resolution, nevertheless, and when she saw her husband, related to him the conversation she had [had] with her sister. Her husband promised to do what he could. Rajmohan had, with the usual bashfulness of boors, chosen the indirect agency of sari government, usually resorted to by poor relatives, instead of a direct and personal application to his brother-in-law. Madhav chose to reply in person, and the next morning drew Rajmohan into a conversation on the subject. He politely enquired what Rajmohan's present pursuits were, and desired to know if he wished to change them. Rajmohan, from foolish pride or shame or perhaps from design, made no avowal of distress, but said he, he had nothing particular to do at present. Madhav then informed him that he had need of the assistance of some able and trustworthy relative to overlook the management of a part of his zemindari, and if Rajmohan had no objection to a change of residence to Radhaganj, he would ask him to do this friendly office.

'That cannot be, sir,' replied Rajmohan; 'with whom can I leave my family?'

'I have thought of that,' replied Madhav. 'I shall provide them with a comfortable home at Radhaganj.'

Rajmohan darted an expression of fierce anger at his brother-in-law.

'At Radhaganj!' he exclaimed. 'Never, I shall sooner die if necessary in prison.' Saying this, he walked away in great anger.

Madhav was surprised at this burst of temper but said nothing. Rajmohan, however, had scarcely a choice to make.

For reasons which even his wife did not know, he had himself become anxious for a change of residence, though Radhaganj he had never thought of. He had made poverty the pretext of his application, but poverty seemed to be the least powerful cause which had led to it. And he also seemed to entertain the utmost repugnance to Madhav's proposal. Taking his chudder Rajmohan left the house. He ran rather than walked through the fields in the noonday sun, stopping nowhere and speaking to nobody. Hours and hours after he returned, with a gloomy and vexed countenance. He had decided on going to Radhaganj with his family, and informed Madhav of his determination in no very gracious terms. Madhav agreed to wait a few days more in Calcutta to allow him to make his preparations, which done they left the city together and reached Radhaganj in a few days.

Notwithstanding the churlish manner with which Rajmohan had accepted of his assistance, Madhav behaved very handsomely towards him. Aware of the unprincipled and unscrupulous character of his rude brother-in-law, but sincerely compassionating the unmerited fate of Matangini, he vested him with the nominal control of one single village but allowed him a handsome salary in return. He also built him a house, the one where this narrative opened, and gave him lands to cultivate by hired labourers if he chose. Indeed, this latter employment chiefly engaged Rajmohan's attention, as he had little or nothing to do with the zemindar's sherista.

But this liberality did not command much gratitude from its [unworthy] object. Ever since their arrival at Radhaganj he behaved with coldness, and perhaps with more than coldness towards his benefactor, and the benefactor and the benefited had little intercourse with each other. Madhav seemed not to notice his strange conduct [or if he] did, it was with indifference, though he never lessened his bounty to its ungrateful object. One painful effect of this feeling on both sides was that the sisters, who loved each other dearly, had very little of each other's company.

A Letter—a Visit to the Zenana

WHEN MADHAV RETURNED FROM HIS GARDEN, WHERE HE HAD parted with his cousin, he found a messenger waiting for him with a letter which he said was '*zaruri*'.[1] Madhav tore it open with eagerness, and devoured its contents. It was from his lawyer at the Sadar station of his district. We will endeavour to give a literal translation of this epistle, interspersing it with the remarks Madhav made as he read.

To sea of glory

Your servant has been engaged in conducting your honour's law-suits at this station, with great carefulness, and hopes that he will succeed in all of them.—

'All of them,' thought Madhav, 'aye, you may say so, lawyer, for my cases are all just. But it is not in the nature of our courts to be right in every case, so I fear, I must take my lawyer's dictum with some allowance. He is an able fellow, however, and manages cases excellently, I must confess.—I heartily wish all this mummery were at an end, but my neighbours must drag me[2] to law. But what next?' The letter proceeded—

It gives me great pain to have to inform you that this day, your aunt has by proxy instituted a suit against you in the principal Sadar Amin Court, alleging that her husband's will is a forgery and claiming the whole estate with *wasilut*.

'My aunt!' exclaimed Madhav in astonishment, the letter dropping from his hands, 'My aunt! She! Heavens! And for

23

my whole Fortune! I a forger. The wretch! I shall kick her out of the house!'

He stood musing for some moments, trembling with rage. But calming himself a little, he picked up the paper and proceeded with it.

I do not know who gave her such counsels, but your servant has made many enquiries, knowing well that someone must have counselled it, and he has heard who it is. Great men are there at her back.

'Counsellors indeed!' thought Madhav 'Who can they be?' He tried to make a guess, first thought of one neighbouring zemindar, then of another, but no one seemed likely, and he resumed reading.

But do not think your honour has anything to fear. The will is in truth real, as I know, and where there is virtue, there is victory. But it is necessary to be very cautious. It would be advisable to give *vakalatnamas* to Babus . . . and vakils of the Judge's Court, as well as to engage another from the Sadar Court on necessary occasions. Barristers from the Supreme Court need also be engaged when the parties join issue as well as at the final hearing. Your servant will do all in his power, and will try for the case even with his life. He waits your honour's orders.

Obedient to orders,
GOKUL CHANDRA DAS.

PS A thousand rupees are at present required to meet necessary expenses.

Madhav's first thought, after he had finished the perusal of the letter was to go and seek his aunt, and to hear what explanation she had to give of her strange proceeding. Madhav therefore immediately hurried into the inner apartments where he found it no very easy task to make himself heard in that busy hour of zenana life. There was a servant woman, black, rotund and eloquent, demanding the transmission to her hands of sundry articles of domestic use, without, however, making it at all intelligible to whom her demands were particularly addressed. There was another, who boasted similar blessed corporal dimensions, but who had thought it beneath her dignity to shelter them from view; and was busily employed, broomstick in hand, in demolishing the little mountains of the skins and stems of sundry culinary vegetables which decorated the floors, and against which the half-naked dame never aimed a blow but coupled it with a curse on those whose duty it had been to prepare the said vegetables for dressing.

A third had ensconced herself in that corner of the yard which formed the grand receptacle of household filth, and was employing all her energies in scouring some brass pots; and as her ancient arms whirled round in rapid evolutions the scarcely less active engine in her mouth hurled dire anathemas against the unfortunate cook, for the mighty reason that the latter had put the said vessels to their legitimate use, and thus caused the labours which excited the worthy matron's ire. The cook herself, far removed from the scene where both her spiritual and her temporal prospects were being so fiercely dealt with by the excited scourer of the brass pots, was engaged in an angry discussion with an elderly lady, apparently the housewife and governess, the subject of debate being no less interesting and important than the quantity of ghee to be allowed her for the culinary purposes of the night. The honest manufacturer of rice and curry was anxious to secure only just double the quantity that was necessary, wisely deeming it advisable that half should be set apart in secret for her own special benefit and consumption. In another corner might be heard those sounds so suggestive of an agreeable supper, the huge *bunti*[3] severing the bodies of fishes doomed to augment the labours of the conscientious cook aforesaid. Several elegant forms might be seen flitting, not often noiselessly but always gracefully, across the *dalans* and veranda with dirty earthen lamps lighted in their little hands, and occasionally sending forth the tinkling of the silver *mall*[4] on their ankles or a summons to another in a voice which surpassed the silver in delicacy. A couple of urchins utterly naked and evidently excrescences in the household, thought the opportunity a fitting one for the display of their belligerent propensities and were making desperate attempts at tearing each other's hair. Some young girls were very clamorously engaged in playing at *agdum bagdum*[5] in the corner of a terrace.

Madhav stood for some moments in utter hopelessness of ever making himself heard in this the veriest of Babels.

'Will you, you wenches,' he cried at length in a key creditable to his lungs, 'will you cease? Can I speak?'

The change this short exclamation produced was magical.[6] The vociferations of the dame whose demands for nameless articles had been hitherto addressed to the air, ceased in the midst of a scream of more than ordinary power, and the black rotund form of the screamer was nowhere to be seen. She of the broomstick threw away the formidable weapon as if stung by an adder, and sought in precipitate flight to shelter her half-naked mass of flesh in the friendly cover of some dark corner. The anathematizing scourer of the brass vessels was cut short in the midst of a very sonorous curse; and both her tongue and her arm were suspended in the middle of half-performed evolutions. The destroyer of the funny tribe also experienced a momentary interruption, but though she mustered courage to resume her task, it was certainly executed with a far smaller expenditure of noise. The presiding divinity of the kitchen abruptly terminated her vocal exertions in favour of ghee and betook to her heels, carrying off in the precipitancy of her flight the entire ghee pot, a bare moiety of which had just formed her demands. The flitting figures with the lit lamps disappeared in tumultuous flight, little caring that the tinkling of the ornaments in their feet betrayed the very presence they endeavoured to conceal. The combat of the sturdy little warriors who fought in nudity and darkness for victory suddenly terminated in flight on both sides, though the abler general of the two did not fail to fire a retiring shot in the shape of a hearty kick at the shins of his antagonist. The little girls too, who had been so merrily playing, rose and followed the said general accompanying him with an ill-suppressed tittle of hilarity. The scene which had just exhibited an unparalleled confusion was suddenly changed into one of utter silence and solitude, and the grave housewife was the only being who stood unmoved and unchanged before the master of the house.

'Masi,' said Madhav, addressing the matron, 'how is this? My house is a very bazaar.'

'Women, son, women,' replied the Masi with a benevolent and affectionate smile, 'it is woman's nature to be screaming.'

'Where is Khuri[7] now, Masi?'

'That is what I was thinking of,' was the reply. 'She has not been seen in the house since morning.'

'Not seen in the house since morning!' exclaimed Madhav in amazement. 'The thing is true then?'

'What is true, son?' replied the maternal aunt.

'Nothing; I will tell you afterwards. Where is she then? Has anyone seen her anywhere?'

'Ambika, Srimati,' cried the matron, addressing the women who were engaged with the fish and the vessels respectively, 'have you seen her anywhere?'

'No,' replied each softly.

'Strange,' said the matron; then, as if addressing the walls, she enquired, 'has anyone seen her?'

'I met her at the Elder House at bathing time,' replied a voice from behind the walls.

'There!' exclaimed the matron in surprise.

'There! In Mathur Dada's house,' exclaimed Madhav also, and then muttered between his teeth, a sudden light flashing upon him, 'cousin Mathur! Can he be the instigator? No, no, it cannot be, I judge wrong.' Then speaking out he said, raising his voice, to one of the women present, 'Go to the Elder House, and see if my aunt is there; if she is, ask her to return, and in case she refuses, know her reasons.'

Midnight Plotting

ALL WHO HAVE THEIR EYES SHUT DO NOT SLEEP. MAT WALLS LIKE stone walls have ears.

Let us now return to Matangini.—Led to her chamber by her aged aunt-in-law after the harsh treatment she had received from her husband, she shut herself up in anguish of spirit. Supper was prepared in due time by the old woman, but not all her requests and entreaties nor those of Kishori, her sister-in-law, could prevail upon her to come out to partake of it. They were obliged therefore to desist and leave her to her own melancholy reflections.

Matangini lay in her bed brooding over the sufferings she was doomed forever to bear. Her husband, she knew, would not see her that night, as was his wont whenever he was offended with her. She, however, felt all the happier for it, and felt a pleasure too in being left alone to indulge in her reflections. The night advanced and one by one the inmates of the house retired to rest. A deep silence pervaded the household as well as all external nature. Matangini's chamber was without a light, and total darkness pervaded it, except where a bright moonbeam that crept through a slight crevice in the small window, streaked the cold mud floor. With her head raised from the pillow and supported on her hand, her *anchal* thrown off from her bosom towards the waist on account of the sultry heat, Matangini gazed on the single ray of moonlight that recalled to her remembrance the days when she could sport beneath the evening beams with the gay and light heart of childhood.

Childhood! That time when she used to lie in the open air, arm in arm with her beloved Hemangini, gazing on the silver orb that poured the sweet light and the interminable deep blue ocean on which she sailed! Many, many were the tales, such as childhood loves, which they then told to each other or heard from their affectionate grandmothers, and hearty was the mirth with which they listened. Eight years had wrought a change. The loud laugh was forgotten, the faces which she loved and whose pictures lay treasured in her heart, she never more could see. And then that smile and that tone of affection! Oh! She could give all she had now in the world again to see that smile, again to hear that tone of human voice. Her heart was a warm spring of inexhaustible love, but it found no vent, and the cold breath of unkindness congealed the celestial stream at its source. One painful remembrance, painful but too sweet in its painfulness not to be brooded over again and again, still connected her past happiness with her present lot. That she wished to forget; but she could not. There was but one human being near her who loved her, the good and guileless Kanak and she alone was mistress of her secret. Beyond this her life was continued misery, and Matangini wept as she thought it could be nothing more.

The sultry heat incident to the season became intolerable, and Matangini rose from her bed to open the window. She was about to open it when the sound of soft and cautious footsteps caught her ear. The sound evidently proceeded from outside the house, and from no distance from the window behind which she stood. The window was, as usual in mat-walled houses, very small, being not more than three feet by two and stood at a height of two feet above the floor. Matangini paused and tried to see through the chink, but could observe nothing beyond a cluster of trees and the far-off tops of others waving against the moonlit sky.

As no footpath lay close to the place whence the sounds of footsteps proceeded, Matangini's apprehensions were excited; she stood motionless, and listened with intense attention. The footsteps approached very close to her and at length ceased; and she could hear whispering voices. Her curiosity was still more strongly excited when she recognized in one of the voices that of her husband, who spoke a little louder than the other. As the mat wall alone divided them, Matangini could catch enough of the sounds, though not all, to be able to understand the meaning of the speaker.

'Why do you speak so loud?' said one of the whisperers, after a few words had been exchanged. 'People in your house may hear us.'

'None can be awake at this hour,' said Rajmohan, as Matangini guessed from the voice.

'Had we not better go a little further off from the wall? Should anyone happen to be awake, she could not then overhear us,' observed the other.

'No,' returned Rajmohan, 'should any be awake as you fear, then we are best as we are, for here under the shadows of the wall and the eaves, no one can possibly see us from the house—neither through the chinks nor probably from outside, should people happen to be out at this hour.'

'True,' said the other, 'but who are in this room here?'

'Why should I tell you that?' Rajmohan said, but immediately addressed, 'There can be no harm in telling it, in my chamber there is nobody there but my wife.'

'Are you sure she is asleep?' demanded the other.

'I think so, but I will go round and see, you wait here.'

Matangini now heard steps receding. Softly and noiselessly she trod the floors and returned to her bed, on which she alighted still more gently and cautiously, so that the least rustling of clothes was not heard. She then threw herself into a posture of sleep, and shut her eyes.

Rajmohan came round to the door of his chamber and lightly tapped at it, nobody came to open it. He called gently to his wife to open the door, but with no better success. He now thought that his wife was really asleep, but thinking it not impossible that she would keep silence from resentment for which he had furnished ample cause, he determined to enter the room anyhow. Rajmohan went to the kitchen, struck a light, and returned with the kitchen lamp in his hand. Then laying it on the ground he applied one foot to one leaf of the door, and held fast the other with an arm. The slack hinges permitted a slight opening to be thus made between the leaves, and Rajmohan thrust a finger in to see if the large bar, the slight wooden bolt, and the little iron chain had all been fastened. He perceived that only the wooden bolt had been used, and rightly judged that his wife had left the door so slightly secured in order to permit him to open it from without if he chose to go in. He easily unfastened the slack bolt by thrusting two fingers in and drawing it aside, and entered the room with the lamp in his hand.

Rajmohan found the features of his wife composed in sleep. He called her several times by name, but so gently as not to awake her; spoke kindly, so that if his wife's silence proceeded from resentment or anger, it might vanish, but still finding her silent and breathing hard, and knowing no reason why she should counterfeit sleep, he was satisfied of its reality and went out, shutting the door after him by the same artifice that had helped him to open it. He then extinguished the lamp, and went round the whole house, tapping at each door and calling in a gentle voice to the slumberers, but finding none awake, rejoined his companion.

As the footsteps of her husband died away, Matangini left her bed and stealing with the same soft tread to the window overheard the following conversation.

After learning from Rajmohan that all was safe, his unknown companion began.

'Are you willing to assist us in this affair?'

'Not much I confess,' said Rajmohan. 'Not that I pretend to be honest so late, but though I don't like the man, he has done me some good.'

'Why then do you not like him?' asked the shrewd stranger.

'Because if he has done me some good he has done me harm too, and perhaps more harm than good,' replied Rajmohan.

'Well, if so, why not assist us?'

'I will, if you give me what I demand. I am anxious to remove from his cursed neighbourhood, but I don't see how I can get food elsewhere without coming to trouble. I wish much therefore to get a sum that will make me care little where I go. If your affair will bring me such an amount of money, I will assist you.'

'Name your condition,' said the stranger.

'First let me know what I am required to do,' responded the other.

'You will do what you have done for us sometimes before this—help us to conceal the property. This time we mean to leave everything we get except cash on your hands, and that this very night.'

'I understand,' Rajmohan replied, 'you will do well not to

conceal from me how much you stand in need of my aid. You are aware that a deed in such a big and wealthy house will be followed by too strict an enquiry and too hot a search for the property to render it convenient to you all to be enjoying your shares in quiet for some time, and you absolutely want somebody who can hold them in trust for you—which you well know none can do so well as I, specially as suspicion will not easily fall on me. Yes, I have an excellent hiding place for such things; but I shall demand too much I fear.'

'You see it—be moderate in your terms,' rejoined the dacoit, for such, the reader sees, he was.

'We won't haggle,' replied Rajmohan. 'I want one-fourth of what you may sell the things for.'

The dacoit knew Rajmohan too well to think he was endeavouring to bully him into a bad bargain.—He was silent for a moment and then said:

'So far as I am concerned—agreed; but I must take the opinion of the others, though you know my word in such matters is their word also.'

'I have no doubt of that,' responded Rajmohan, 'but one word more. Before you take away those things, we will make a guesswork of what the things will sell for—and you will pay me down a fourth of it in cash. Of course I shall afterwards make up for anything that may fall short of expectation, and you will do the same to me if you get more.'

'Certainly it will be so, but one word to you also.—You are to do another service.'

'I will, if you name another price.'

'Yes, of course. We mean to carry off Madhav Ghose's property for ourselves; but we want to carry off something else for another.'

'What?' enquired Rajmohan with some show of curiosity.

'His uncle's will.'

'*Hoon*,' exclaimed Rajmohan starting slightly.

'Yes—and will be paid for it. Now we want to know from you where Madhav keeps that will.'

'I don't know it exactly myself. I have seen him take out his document from a certain box, but I don't know where that box is kept, whether he keeps it in another box or chest or almirah, I know nothing—but who pays you for the will?'

'I am bound not to tell.'

'Not even to me?'

'To none.'

'Is it Mathur Ghose?'

'May be or may not—but what sort of a box is it?'

'The terms?'

'What do you ask?'

'Two hundred in cash.'

'Rather too much for two or three words. But we have too much to do'—the dacoit continued, speaking more to himself than to the other, 'to be searching for a bit of paper all night. The box must be in some iron chest in the bedroom; so we can find it easily if we only know what sort of box contains it. There is no jabbering with you—so be it as you say.'

'It is an ivory box,' Rajmohan said, 'with three English letters written in gold on the lid. Those are the first letters of his name.'

'So now that it is arranged,' said the dacoit, 'come with me and let us see our men. We will appoint a place of rendezvous where you will wait for us. Come, there is no time to lose; the work must be commenced as soon as the moon sets, and summer nights are short.'

So saying the robber and his confederate softly stole from the shadow of the wall and took their way towards the woods at a distance from each other, soon to reunite in another dark spot. Matangini sank on the floor in astonishment and dismay.

Love Can Conquer Fear[1]

In which the author narrowly misses an opportunity of introducing a few ghosts and regrets that he cannot gratify his young readers.

EVERY WORD THAT CAUGHT THE EAR OF MATANGINI FROZE HER with horror during the terrible dialogue she overheard. As long as it continued, the intense interest with which she listened sustained her trembling frame, but so soon as it was ended, she sank overpowered on the floor. For some moments she remained almost insensible from the stupor of fear and agony. By degrees she recovered composure enough to think on what she had heard. A new and terrible light had just been thrown on the life and character of her husband. She had hitherto known him as a man of mad heart and brutal temper, but she recoiled with horror at the recollection that the accomplice of robbers, himself a robber perhaps, had hitherto enjoyed her innocent bosom. And the future? Was it in her power, now that her eyes were opened, to tear herself from his disgusting embraces? No, no, she was forever cursed!

Such thoughts would rend her bosom at one moment—at the next the daring crime to which he was going to lend a hand burst on her sight with fearful vividness. She trembled as she thought of this. And the victims of this horrible deed were to be her own Hemangini and her Madhav. Her hair stood on end, her blood tingled in her veins, and a sharp pang shot across her head. All thoughts of her own accursed future and

degraded womanhood vanished as she thought of the beloved
beings who were now sleeping in fancied security while utter
poverty and misery, perhaps worse, yawned to engulf them
in an hour. She felt she must save them if she could, even at
the price of her life.

Her first thought was to alarm her own household. But the
next moment she perceived the folly of the thought. Who in the
household would believe it of Rajmohan? Would his aunt believe
it? Or would his sister? Most probably they would think her
crazed, delirious or dreaming. And supposing they did believe,
would they endanger Rajmohan to save Madhav? And even if
they would, could they save him? No, they dreaded too much
their formidable relative to act in the slightest manner against
his wishes. And should they not believe her, but in any manner
let him know what she had uttered, her doom would be sealed.

She next thought of Kanak. Might not Kanak be sent to
inform Madhav's household? Kanak's house was close by and
Matangini might steal away from her chamber and awaken
and impart to her so much of what she knew as would suffice
to warn Madhav without endangering Rajmohan. But this course
also appeared unpromising, if not impossible. She could not
awaken Kanak without awakening Kanak's mother also, for
both she knew, slept in the same room. Kanak might perhaps
believe anything she said without asking for explanations, but
Kanak's mother would not. To satisfy her it would be necessary
to reveal everything and implicate her husband, but Matangini
could not for all the world turn informer against the man to
whom she had pledged her faith before God and man. Nor
would it be possible to impart to Kanak alone the purpose of
a midnight visit, and would Kanak's mother allow her daughter
to leave her home at midnight, alone, or what she perhaps

might think as bad, in the company of another young woman? Far from it, it was rather more likely that she would awaken Matangini's household in return, and deliver her over to their custody, fairly making it certain that Matangini had become either mad or dishonest. And even with her mother's consent, would Kanak have the courage to venture on such a journey at such an hour unattended or attended by only another woman, herself, specially when bands of dacoits were out, lurking on the wayside?

Matangini now perceived with despair that her only resource lay in herself. She must go herself. Her whole soul recoiled at the idea. She thought not of the danger, though the danger was great. At this hour of dread loneliness, a young woman would have to thread her way through a wild and jungly path. She was, naturally enough, superstitious and her rich imagination was stored with tales of unearthly haunters of the woods, and had fed on them since infancy. A band of desperate robbers were stationed somewhere in the vicinity, and should she fall into their hands, she shuddered to think what might be the consequence. If among these robbers she should meet her husband! Matangini shuddered again.

Matangini had a brave heart, and for her sister and her husband she felt she could risk her life.

As the appalling dangers rose before her mind, her noble love expanded and rose also, and she longed to sacrifice at its altar a life whose burden her crushed heart could not[2] longer bear. But still another womanly feeling kept her back. To go to the house of Madhav at midnight and alone! Who would understand her? What would Madhav think! She pressed her brows and stood thinking in an unmoved attitude.

Undecided she heaved a deep sigh, and to relieve herself of

the heat that oppressed her, she ventured to open the little window. The trees now cast shadows of huge length and the moon hung over the far horizon, shedding a waning light. In an hour she would vanish, the loud shout of the robbers would be heard, 'and then,' thought Matangini, 'it will be too late to save them.' The near approach of certain danger banished her scruples, her love returned with tenfold energy, and she no longer hesitated.

Wrapping herself in a coarse piece of bedcloth from head to foot she gently opened the door, and issuing out of the chamber, closed it with the same care and drew the bolt after her in the same manner as Rajmohan had done. As she stood out in the open space and eyed the vast solitude of the blue heavens and the thick mass of the noiseless tops of the trees, her heart again misgave [her] and her feet refused their office. 'Gods, give me strength,' she uttered with her hands clasped on her bosom. Then summoning all her resolutions, she made rapid but noiseless steps. Her heart beat as she walked through the jungly path. The dreary silence and the dark shadows appalled her. The knotted trunks of huge trees showed like so many unearthly forms watching her progress in malignant silence. In each leafy bough that shot over her darkened path, she fancied there lurked a demon. In each dark recess she could see the skulking form and glistening eyes of a spectre or of a robber. All the wild tales she had heard of fierce visages and ghostly grins that had appalled to death the belated traveller, rushed to her imagination. The light rack of the falling leaf, the flapping wings of some frightened nightbird as it changed its unseen seat among the dark branches, the slight rustle of crawling reptiles among the fallen leaves, even her own footsteps made her heart

fainter and fainter. Still the resolute girl hurried on, taking
the name of her patron goddess a thousand times within her
heart, and now and then muttering a prayer. The darkest part
of the path wound along a glade which lay between two plots
of raised ground. On one side was a vast mango *tope*[3] enclosed
by a high and impervious hedge of prickly vegetation. On
the other side was the raised bank of a pool covered with
underwood above which waved the vast foliage of three
bur[4] trees, darkening the footpath which wound beneath
their shadows. Matangini cast around her eyes in fear. From
the middle of the mango tope issued a strong glare of light,
and she could even hear low discordant voices. All her worst
fears were realized. There was the robber band. Matangini
stood chained to the spot, unable to move a step. To add to her
misfortune a dog which lay by the wayside rose up and began
to bark loudly at the sight of a passenger at night. Immediately
the voices in the garden were hushed. Matangini still retained
presence of mind enough to see that the dacoits had taken the
warning given by the animal, and that she was likely soon to
be discovered. Danger again restored her energies. Darting
with the fleetness and the lightness of the gazelle across the
darkened bank of the pool, she as swiftly ascended to the edge
of the water. Her position was now concealed by the bank
from the view of any who might look for her in the footpath;
but should the robbers think of looking about the bank on
which the bur trees stood, she was lost. No bush or thicket
was near to afford her a shelter. Her energies had been roused
and she did not lose a moment. The dog still barked. She
hastily loosened a heavy clod of earth from the moist edge
of the water, placed it in the coarse cloth in which she had
wrapped herself, and tied it in a bundle, so that it might

not float when thrown into the water. Thus prepared to free
herself from an incumbrance[5] which might betray her, for the
light sari could be managed with ease, she stood ready for an
emergency. Footsteps could now be distinctly heard and voices
whispered on the other side of the bank. She gently sank
the bundle in the water, taking care that the water might not
splash. Then as gently gliding into the water at a spot where
the spreading branches of the bur cast a deep shadow, she
sat down immersed to her chin, so that nothing but her head
was visible, if indeed it could be seen where the dark water of
the pool was made darker by the sombre shade of the tree.
But still apprehensive lest the fair complexion of her lily
face [should] betray her, she unloosed the knot of her hair
and spread the dark luxuriant tresses on all sides of her head,
so that not even the closest scrutiny could now distinguish
from above the dark hair floating over the darkened pool.

Presently the footsteps and the whispering voices approached
this side of the bank and descended halfway. Matangini could
hear this, but did not turn her head.

'It is strange,' said one of the voices within her hearing, 'I
thought I saw through an opening in the hedge a figure wrapped
in a chudder standing on the pathway.'

'You must have mistaken a tree for a man,' said the
other, 'for could any have disappeared so soon? Besides, would
any sane man wrap himself in a thick chudder as you say, in
this season?'

'Yes, you may be right,' was the reply, 'or it might be an
apadevata[6] that I have seen.'

She too gave a last glance around them, without discovering,
however, the timid intruder who formed the cause of their
apprehension. They then walked away.

Matangini waited in the water for some minutes even after she had heard the last audible sound of their footsteps, and when she thought they had regained the mango grove, she came out of her watery shelter and gently squeezed the water out of her sari, abandoning to it the lost chudder. Without venturing again on the dangerous footpath above, she took her way along the edge of the water, along a bank at right angles to the one she had left, casting looks of anxious fear behind her. She knew well the footpaths here, for though so strictly forbidden the Madhumati, she had permission to resort to this piece of water for her daily ablutions. From this bank the fair adventurer cut across a little footpath which she knew led through a dense mass of underwood to the one that she had been compelled to desert. It was at length gained, though not without repeated misgivings of the heart. There she stood at a distance from the mango grove and the animal which had caused her so much trouble. But a new difficulty threatened to check her further progress. Since her arrival at Radhaganj she had but twice visited her sister, and never on foot, but closed in a *palki*. As much of the way as she knew from hearsay she had passed, but now her footsteps rested at the intersecting point of crossroads. Bewildered by her new difficulty, she turned her eyes on all directions and luckily caught sight of the tops of the tall *devdaru* trees which she knew stood in front of Madhav's house. She immediately struck the path which led in that direction and soon got the huge edifice in view, towards the *khirki* or postern gate of which she turned her steps.

[The last difficulty had yet to be overcome. All in the household were asleep at that hour, and it was after knocking a good many times that she succeeded in rousing Karuna, the maidservant of the house.]

'Who knocks at this time of night?' enquired Karuna surlily.

'Oh hasten, hasten, Karuna, open the door,' cried Matangini anxiously.

'But who are you that I shall open the door to you at this time of night?' again demanded Karuna in the same surly tone, indignant that the sweetness of her repose should be disturbed by an untimely intruder.

'Come, come soon—you will see,' said Matangini in a beseeching tone, unwilling to speak out who she was.

'But who are you?' cried Karuna more furiously than ever.

'I am a woman and no thief, come and see,' was the reply.

It struck the slowly opening senses of Karuna that a thief does not usually possess so sweet a voice as the one she heard. Without further parley, therefore, she came to the door and opened it.

'You, Thakurani!'[7] exclaimed Karuna in utter astonishment at beholding Matangini.

'I want to see my sister,' said the latter. 'Lead me to her.'

But Karuna's faculties had scarcely recovered from her surprise, and the worthy dame kept on asking questions.

'You here!' she repeated, 'and at midnight! What brings you here, mother? Your clothes are wet. What has happened?'

The impatient girl replied not to her questions, but said again in a commanding tone, 'Lead me to my sister.'

'She is asleep,' said Karuna, 'yet we will awaken her. But wait, first change your clothes.'

'Give me a sari soon if you can, or lead on.'

Karuna gave her a sari that was at hand, and Matangini changing her light apparel in a trice followed Karuna to the apartments above stairs.

Forewarned and Forearmed

MATANGINI STOPPED AT AN OPEN VERANDA AND DESIRED KARUNA
to awaken her sister and bring her thither. In a few minutes
Hemangini, who had not been asleep, came with utter
astonishment depicted in her face and enquired in an eager
tone the object of her unexpected and untimely visit.

'I come to warn,' said Matangini, 'there will be a dacoity
in your house.'

'Dacoity!' half screamed, half muttered the astounded girl.

'*Hem!*'[1] shrieked Karuna.

'Softly, Karuna,' said Matangini, 'gently Hem; why stand
you here? Go warn your husband and bid him be prepared.'

But Hemangini was then utterly unfit for the task. She
stood pale and trembling, unable either to answer or move.
Matangini was perplexed, she saw that her sister was lost in
fear and time could not be spared. The loquacious zeal of
Karuna, who could not for the world forego[2] this opportunity
of being the first to carry such dreadful tidings, as well as
the salutary effect that had been produced upon her fears by the
unexpected intelligence, relieved Matangini of her anxiety, and
the mortal enemy of the finny[3] tribe, big with the importance
of being the messenger of evil, flew to Madhav's chamber to
discharge the mission which legitimately belonged to Hemangini.

She soon returned and informed Matangini that Madhav
did not feel disposed to give weight to her (Karuna's) words
and seemed particularly incredulous when she said that
Matangini was in the house and that it was she who had brought

45

the intelligence. 'If she is here,' Madhav had said, 'I can hear the news from herself; bring her to me that I may learn from my sister-in-law how much there is to fear. Ask her to come hither.'

'Go Hem,' said Matangini to her sister. 'You go—tell your husband that I am here and that what I say is true. He will believe you.'

'No, no,' said the girl, 'you must go yourself. How can I answer all the questions that he may ask? Go—answer all the questions that he may ask. Go and lose no time, for if it be as you say—'

'I had better not go. Tell him that I say it, and that it is true.'

'No—you go,' again urged the reluctant girl with sweet childlike obstinacy.

'I *cannot* go, I must not,' said Matangini in the most serious tone and in an agitated voice.

'O Luck!' shouted Karuna laughingly. 'It is nothing then? Your sister wants to frighten you only, mother.'

'Ah! Sister, do you want to frighten me only?' said Hemangini her face brightening. 'I confess I am frightened— now tell me what is your errand.'

Matangini mused in deep silence for a minute; then taking her resolution, she said, 'Yes, I will go to him. You come with me, Hem.'

But the modest girl positively refused to appear before her husband in the presence of her sister, though she did not say as much in words. 'Stay then and speak not a word about me or my errand till I come back,' said Matangini and darted away through the veranda, for she saw the moon's disk sinking on the tops of the trees. But as Matangini neared the door of Madhav's apartment, her feet trembled more violently than even when she had stood eyeing the glaring light in the mango grove. She drew her sari over her forehead and proceeded softly and with seeming reluctance. She receded, advanced, stopped short, pushed aside the door, stopped again, and at length entered. A single lamp illuminated the gaily decorated apartment and the young Babu reclined on a rich sofa. Matangini stationed herself close to a wall with downcast head as befitted the modesty of her sex and age, her face scarcely turned towards that of her brother-in-law. Madhav gave a start and then only half rose from his reclining posture.

Neither, however, spoke, although one was as anxious to impart the fearful tidings she bore as the other to receive them, and a silence ensued which evidently embarrassed both. At length Madhav spoke jestingly, as the connection between them authorized.

'I wish you were an English Memshahib, sister-in-law,' said he with a smile, 'that I might offer you a seat. But why not sit down on—on—'

Matangini relieved him from his embarrassment by saying almost in a whisper, 'Have you heard what I have to say?'

'Yes,' said Madhav seriously, 'is it true?'

'It is true,' she said in the same half-audible tone.

'Tonight you say?'

'Tonight, even now they will make their attack as soon as the moon sinks and the moon will sink in half a *danda*.'[4]

'Is it? Then I am lost. But how do you know all this, sister-in-law?'

'That,' replied Matangini in a more distinct voice, slightly lifting the cloth which covered her forehead, 'that you must not ask me.'

'You perplex me,' rejoined he. 'I scarcely know what to

think.' Matangini now completely uncovered her face and looking steadily into his, spoke in a yet bolder tone. 'Do you not know me, Madhav? Can I deceive you? And do you think I would come to your house, at this hour, and unattended—'

'Sure—I was wrong,' he answered, 'wait here with your sister while I go and rouse my men.'

Matangini arrested him with a look as he was rising and asked him to give her one word more.

'What is it?' he asked.

'Where is your uncle's will—take care of it—they mean to carry it off.'

'Humph,' ejaculated Madhav, a sudden light flashing upon him as he called to mind his aunt's lawsuit. 'They shall not have it.'

'Do you not keep it in an ivory box in this room?'

'Yes—how do you know it?' he enquired in fresh amazement.

'Why I? They know it,' she replied.

'Now I see it! he answered. 'You must be too well informed,' and he rose to depart.

'I have something to beg of you—will you grant it?'

'Ask it and it will be yours.'

'Then say not a word to a human being that I have been your informant or even that I have been here tonight; my life depends on it.'

'How your life? Who dares threaten it?' exclaimed he with a flash of indignation.

'Hush!' said she.

'Yes, I forget!' said he checking himself. 'I promise you silence.'

'And impose the same on Karuna and my sister as you go.'

'With Karuna, it will be rather difficult, but I shall frighten the wench into dumbness. You stop with your sister, with closed doors and you will remain here unperceived by the household. When I come back I shall lead you to a place of greater security and privacy.'

So saying he passed by his wife and Karuna, each of whom he desired or commanded to be strictly silent regarding Matangini. Then darting swiftly into the outer department,[5] he was at once in the midst of his *darwans*.

Madhav knew Matangini to be a woman of too clear a mind to have been greatly deceived, and he knew her also too well to think she would ever be at so much pains to deceive him. He therefore set himself to the work of preparation in earnest. Before total darkness had covered the face of the earth, the house-top might be seen full of human forms flitting against the sky. These were select men from the tenantry who lived close to the house and from among whom a little *lattial* force could be collected at any time at a moment's notice. These were mostly armed with *latties*,[6] spears, bricks and other missiles ready to be hurled at the doomed invader that durst approach the walls or enter the house. We do not pretend to say that all these midnight warriors bore a heart as sturdy as the latties that they clasped in their hands, and many doubtless there were who thought this untimely interruption of their repose very unwelcome, and who would have gladly beat a retreat did not the stern voice of their landlord, as it rolled forth command after command, convince them that it would be safer to stay and trust to chance than risk his displeasure. Most, however, felt secure in their position; there was but little [in the] house on the top, to tempt the steps of robbers, and with this comfortable assurance the bold defenders stood boldly by their posts. Five or six men of the sturdier race from the North-west protected the entrance, well accoutred with sword, shield, spear and musket. Four or five others could be seen walking round, with orders to be on the alert, and to give the warning when necessary to the rest. Inside the house, the boxes and chests which contained the most valuable things, jewels, cash, plate and other articles of small bulk and great value, as also the coveted ivory box, were nowhere to be seen. They were removed to obscure hiding places which among the endless apartments of the ample edifice could never be [discovered] by one who had never seen them, and it was not everyone of the inmates of the house that had a knowledge of their existence. Madhav was everywhere mild and easily yielding by nature under ordinary circumstances; his energy and activity in the moment of excitement was feverish and held in awe the timid and the hesitating. Nevertheless not few were the women, who dragging naked children in one arm and holding large wallets under the other, stealthily left the threatened house to seek shelter in the neighbouring huts, whose humble pretensions protected them from the chance of spoliation. Among the fleetest and foremost might be seen the conscientious cook who had signalized[7] herself by victory in the preceding evening, and who now conducted a most dexterous retreat with bag and baggage, not forgetting the famous ghee pot which formed the glorious trophy of her evening triumph.

The hum and bustle of preparation subsided as all [was] completed and the expectant crowd awaited the issue in silence. The moon had already set and Madhav began half to doubt the truth of Matangini's suspicions. Just as his thoughts were taking that direction a darwan came up to him and informed him in Hindi that one of the men appointed to keep a lookout, had seen a light in the direction of the 'old garden' (as the mango grove where Matangini had nearly encountered the robbers was called) and that venturing in that direction very close to the grove he had observed [several] armed men assembled in that place. 'What is [your command,]' asked the man, 'shall we go and attack [them]?'

['Hurry] not, Bhup Sing,' replied Madhav, 'it is unnecessary, and besides if you go in insufficient numbers, you will be overpowered, but if on the other hand many of you go, you leave the house unprotected, and who knows but there may be another company?'

'Is it Maharaj's pleasure, then, we remain as we are?' asked the darwan.

'Yes—but set up a shout all of you together, and let the rascals perceive how well prepared we are.'

No sooner had he spoken than a long loud shout rent the midnight air. The females trembled in their apartments as they listened in awe and thought the danger near. A dismal silence succeeded the noise.

'Another shout—once more,' said Madhav.

Again a similar sound shook the night. No sooner had its echoes died away, than out rose a terrific yell from the wilderness, as if uttered by midnight demons who revelled in the dark. The blood ran cold in the veins of the listeners as the horrible sound fell on their ears.

'Again, again, my men, once more [raise] your voices, and louder than ever,' shouted Madhav, apprehensive lest the appalling sound chilled the courage of his retainers. Again was the order obeyed with zeal and promptness, and again arose a responsive cry from the direction of the 'old garden'. But this time it was the cooing cry known among robbers as the signal of retreat.

'They fly; they fly; they fly,' shouted several voices, 'that is the cry of flight.'

'Yes, but do not be too sure,' said Madhav, 'it may have been uttered to deceive you. Remain as you are.'

Long did Madhav and his men wait, but nothing occurred. After another injunction to his retainers not to relax their vigilance and to keep up all night, Madhav turned his steps towards the inner apartments to thank the brave woman who had saved him from imminent danger.

We Meet to Part

'CAN I EVER FORGET WHAT YOU HAVE DONE FOR ME?' SAID Madhav to Matangini, after he had rejoined his wife and his sister-in-law. The former, as soon as her heart was relieved of its load of apprehensions, lightly tripped out of the room leaving her sister alone with him. 'Can I ever forget what you have done?' said Madhav looking more gratitude than he expressed in words.

'If you cannot, let it be for Hem's sake that you remember it. Should she ever fall under your displeasure, which Heavens forbid! may the memory of her sister's sufferings obtain her pardon! As for myself, I could not do otherwise than I have done it—I will take leave of you.'

'Why, sister-in-law?' returned Madhav. 'Your sister has not seen you long—she will be overjoyed to be with you for a few hours more. When it is day, my palki will convey you to your home, if you cannot longer remain. Why depart tonight and on foot?'

'Fate rules it otherwise. That happiness I must forgo,' returned she sadly; 'I must go.'

'Why sister-in-law, why so?' asked Madhav again. 'Cannot your sister's husband know the reason?'

'*He!*' said she, as much with shame as with sorrow. 'You know *him* well. He will be angry if I remain.'

'Angry if you remain with your sister?' again enquired Madhav. 'Did you promise him to return so soon? Does he know where you are?'

'No,' said she, 'I did not promise him anything, nor does he know where I am.'

'Strange,' said Madhav, 'I don't understand how then you could come. Was he at home when you left?'

'Ask not such questions,' replied she.

A dark suspicion crossed Madhav's mind at this reply,[1] but he soon abandoned it as groundless. He sat musing in deep silence for moments during which Matangini kept fixed on him her large, blue, sorrowful eyes.

'Why do I linger?' she said at length. 'I go; Karuna will go with me. Farewell,' added she sadly, her voice growing thick. 'Fare you well! Be you happy, Madhav.' Madhav looked up to her face—it was wet; Matangini was weeping! 'And be my Hem happy with you.'

'You weep!' said Madhav. 'You are unhappy.'

Matangini replied not, but sobbed. Then, as if under the influence of a maddening agony of soul, she grasped his hands in her own and bending over them her lily face so that Madhav trembled under the thrilling touch of the delicate curls that fringed her spotless brow, she bathed them in a flood of warm and gushing tears.

'Ah, hate me not, despise me not,' cried she with an intensity of feeling which shook her delicate frame.[2] 'Spurn me not for this last weakness; this, Madhav, this, may be our last meeting; it must be so, and too, too deeply have I loved you—too deeply do I love you still, to part with you forever without a struggle.'

Did Madhav chide her? Ah, no! He covered his eyes with his palm and his palm became wet with rears. There was a deep silence for some moments, but their hearts beat loud. Matangini, recovering her presence of mind as speedily as she had lost it, first broke the heart-rending silence.

The distant and reserved demeanour, the air of dejection and broken-heartedness which had marked her from the first, had disappeared; the impetuosity and fervour of the first burst of a deep and burning love had subsided; and Matangini now stood calm and serene, her usually melancholy features beaming with the light of an unutterable feeling. A sweet and sober pensiveness still mantled her tender features, but it was not the pensiveness of deep-felt enjoyment, for the wild current of passion had hurried her to that region where naught but the present was visible, and in which all knowledge of right and wrong is whirled and merged in the vortex of intense present felicity. Was not Matangini now in Madhav's presence? And had not her long-pent-up tears fallen on his hands? Had he not wept with her? That was all Matangini remembered, and for a moment the memory of duty, virtue, principle ceased to fling its sombre shadow on the brightness of the impure felicity in which her heart [revelled]. There was a fire in that voluptuous eye,—there was a glow on that moonbeam brow, and as she stood leaning with her well-rounded arm on the damask-covered back of the sofa, her beautiful head resting on the palm of her hand over which, as over the heaving bosom, strayed the luxuriant tresses of raven hue;—as thus she stood, Madhav might well have felt sure earth had not to show a more dazzling vision of female loveliness.

'I had thought,' she cried at length in a voice which trembled from emotion, 'I had thought that never again would human ears, not even your own, hear from my lips the language I breathed tonight, ah! I know not what I felt.'

'Matangini,' said Madhav, speaking for the first time since the storm of passion had burst, 'I too had thought we could part without a struggle, but you have—you see what you have done. But,' continued he, his eyes again suffused with tears, 'you have made many sacrifices, make one last sacrifice. Root out the feeling from a heart on which no impurity should leave a spot. Forget.'

'Blame me not,' she said, and then interrupting herself, she bent down her head to hide the tear that gushed again with the current of feeling. 'Yes, reproach me, Madhav,' she continued, 'censure me, teach me, for I have been sinful; sinful in the eyes of my God, and I must say it, Madhav, of my God on earth, of yourself. But you cannot hate me more than I hate myself. Heaven alone knows what I have felt—felt for the long long years that have passed, could I rip open this heart you could then and then only know how it beats.'

Madhav wept again. 'Matangini dear, beloved Matangini—' he began, but his voice thickened, and he could not proceed.

'Oh say again, again say those words, words that my heart has yearned to hear—say Madhav, do you then love me still? Oh! Say but once again and tonight I shall meet death with happiness.'

'Listen to me, Matangini,' replied Madhav, scarcely cool himself, 'listen and spare both of us this sore affliction. At your father's house the flame was kindled which seems fated to consume us both and which then we were too young to quench by desperate efforts, but if even then we never flinched from the path of duty, shall we not, now that years of affliction have schooled our hearts, eradicate from them the evil which corrodes and blisters them? Oh! Matangini, let us forget each other. Let us separate.' And Madhav heaved a sigh.

Matangini rose and stood erect in the splendour of new flushed beauty. 'Yes,' said she with desperate effort, 'if the human mind can be taught to forget, I will forget you. We part now and forever,' and there was desperate calmness in her voice.

Pulling her veil over her face to hide the stream that again welled forth from her eyes in spite of her efforts, Matangini hurriedly left the room.

The Return

IT WANTED AN HOUR TO THE FIRST STREAKS OF DAYBREAK, when Matangini with sad heart and heavy steps again threaded the wild footpath. Karuna silently followed her homeward footsteps. The paling blue of the starry heavens was now half covered by numbers of driving clouds, while one dense and settled mass of black hovered over the distant horizon and shed a sombre grey over the dimly seen outlines of the far-off treetops on its verge. A wild and fitful breeze occasionally moaned over the dark woods with an ominous sound and a few drops of pattering rain fell on the earth, on the leafy trees and on the luxuriant shrubbery. Matangini was too deeply absorbed in her own thoughts to heed the appearance of external nature, though lowering and gloomy looked the scene around her. The remembrance of the forbidden and fond interview she had just stolen, engrossed all her soul; not even the thoughts of the reception which might await her at home, not even the risk and danger of discovery by her husband, obliterated the faintest tint of the vivid picture which memory of fancy successfully traced before her mental view, now in the darkest, now in the most radiant colours. She had promised to forget; the first thing she did after leaving Madhav was to remember; to remember and hang with rapture on each word he had uttered,—on each tear he had shed; and often would the rapture vanish and be succeeded by the thought that god and man abhorred her impurity of heart.

A part of their journey had been accomplished when the growing blackness of the skies announced that a storm was near.

'Thakurani, hasten your footsteps,' said Karuna, breaking the long silence; 'there will be a storm; let us reach your house before it commences.'

'Yes,' said Matangini unconsciously, 'go on.'

Karuna increased her speed and Matangini imitated her, more from example than from any sense of necessity.

'There—hear—bigger drops are falling on the leaves,' said Karuna speaking once more.

'Yes?' said Matangini, then awaking for the first time from her abstraction, and, stopping to listen, continued, 'Ah it is not the sound of raindrops—it seems to be—what? Perhaps the sound of human feet treading over the leaves and stumps of trees.'

'Is it so, Thakuran?' ejaculated Karuna and increased her speed, apprehensive lest she should fall into the hands of some loiterer from among the dacoit band.

But they had not proceeded far when the wind rose in fury, the lightning flashed, the thunder growled, and big drops of rain poured down too unmistakably.

'We shall be drenched to death,' said Karuna. 'Can we not shelter ourselves beneath this tree?'

'Come then,' said Matangini, as she led the way to the cover afforded by the overspreading boughs of a large tamarind. Just then a sudden flash of light illuminated the earth and revealed by its momentary gleam a human figure standing at the foot of the tree, within speaking distance of themselves.

'Fly, O fly!' shrieked Karuna, and waiting not for an answer, ran with all her might, dragging the nerveless Matangini after her as she sped away. 'Fly, fly, fly,' she kept on crying and ran on amidst the storm and rain and stopped not to take breath till she had reached the house which fortunately was nigh.

'Stay here not,' said Matangini after they had arrived there, 'although it is cruel to turn you out at this hour—it will be more dangerous for you to stay, cross over to Kanak's, and remain there in the veranda; when the storm abates a little and the daylight comes you can leave the house before the family arise from their beds.'

So saying, Matangini proceeded to open the door of her sleeping apartment, and Karuna left the house. Matangini found the door still shut, and unbarring it by the same artifice which Rajmohan had used a few hours before, she gently entered the apartment. She was in the act of shutting the door again when another figure glided into the room after her and drew the massive bar. The very sound of the tread of his feet told Matangini that it was her dreaded husband.

Rajmohan said nothing, but by feeling in the dark he brought out a tinder box and with flint and steel struck a light and placed it on its accustomed seat. Still he spoke not but sat on the *taktaposh* or bedstead, eyeing his wife with a savage glance. Matangini read her fate in his looks and stood, not pale and trembling but firmly and proudly, with all the dignity and courage which had that very evening awed into silence the fury of her brutal oppressor. The howling of the wind and the clatter of the rain without, and the angry growl in the clouds above were the only sounds that disturbed the appalling silence.

At length Rajmohan spoke, 'Accursed woman,' he said in a bitter tone which had in it nothing of the unusual savage impetuosity of his temper, 'did you not go to your paramour?'

Matangini did not answer. 'Speak,' he said in a low voice of fearful imperiousness, stamping his foot on the ground.

'I shall not answer to questions which I ought not to be asked,' replied the half-guilty and half-innocent woman.

'Wretch,' exclaimed Rajmohan, gnashing his teeth and growing furious; but again assuming a forced calmness, he added, 'did you or did you not go to Madhav Ghose's home this night?'

'Yes, I did,' she said, suddenly excited beyond herself by the sound of the name, 'I did—to save him from the robbery you had planned.'

Rajmohan sprang from the bed with clenched fists.

'Woman,' he said fiercely, 'deceive me not. Canst thou?[1] Thou little knowest how I have watched thee; how from the earliest day that thy beauty became thy curse, I have followed every footstep of thine—caught every look that shot from thine eyes. Brute though I be,' continued he again becoming gentle, 'I was proud of my beautiful wife and as the tigress watches over her whelp, I watched over thee. Did I not perceive how before thou wert a woman, thou didst already become fond of that cursed wretch? Did I not see how time ripened thy fondness into sin? Doubt thou what I say? Know then that this very afternoon, when won by the poisoned words of that harlot, thy friend, thou didst leave the house unbidden, thou didst not leave unwatched. Then too I was behind thee— I was behind thee—deny it woman, if thou canst, when before the garden thou didst wilfully, yea most wickedly—most treacherously, let go thy veil, why?[2] That your eyes might meet—and be blasted! Once and once only I missed thee— and I rue the hour when I did so. But returning at night to my untenanted chamber could I not guess the serpent's hole into which the vile worm had crept? I did and watched thee again at his khirki gate. Knowest not that in the moaning wind and amidst the howling storm I have dogged thy steps even but now?—knowest thou, harlot, why I have whetted my knife tonight? You answer not and I ask not for answer. I will kill you.' He ceased and his eyes darted fire as he cast a last glance of scrutiny over her petrified features. A momentary pause ensued during which the howling storm without was alone heard. At length Matangini spoke and desperate calmness was in her voice.

You are right,' she said. 'I love him—deeply do I love him; long loved I and I love him so. I will also tell you that words have I uttered which, but for the uncontrolled—uncontrollable madness of a love you cannot understand, would never have passed these lips. But beyond this I have not been guilty to you. Do you believe me?'

'No,' said he, rising from his seat. 'I will kill you.' And he unsheathed a small dagger that hung from his waist concealed in his clothes.

'My mother, O mother! And you father! Where are you now?' were the only sounds that escaped the lips of the doomed girl, as she sunk about lifeless on the floor.[3] The ruthless weapon gleamed high, as it was about to descend on the lovely bosom of the trembling victim, when the purpose was suddenly arrested by a violent noise at the window. Rajmohan turned round to see the cause of the unexpected noise. The *jhamp*[4] flew open and two dark and athletic forms sprang one after another into the chamber, dripping with rain and bespattered with mud, but shooting sparks of fire from their red and fierce glances.

When Thieves Fall Out

In which is discussed the physical possibility of a robber being robbed and an assassin assassinated.

'YOU THINK OF KILLING YOUR WIFE, RUFFIAN?' SAID ONE OF THE newcomers, who, however, had not come with any peaceful intentions himself as his heavy arms and gleaming dagger showed.

'Who are you?' roared Rajmohan, turning all his fury towards the intruders, and brandishing his knife with fearful rapidity. 'Burglary in my house!'

'Softly, the inmates in the other rooms will be aroused. No thieves, friend. Look well and possibly you may recognize me,' responded one of the newcomers with a contemptuous smile. 'Lass,' continued he addressing Matangini, 'bring that lamp here that your husband may have a look at the face of a friend.'

But Matangini, though not absolutely senseless, had fallen into a stupor—so bewildering had been the attack on her life and so strange the scarcely less fearful interruption that followed it.

'Friend or foe,' said Rajmohan, 'go out of my house.'

'That you may murder your wife in quiet?' said the intrepid stranger with a sarcastic laugh.

'And who will prevent me from doing it if I choose?' exclaimed the furious husband, and dagger in hand rushed to plunge it in the audacious visitor's breast. But quick as lightning the latter parried the blow, and then with one stroke of his own gleaming sabre he made that tiny weapon in Rajmohan's hand fly off to a distance of several feet. Losing not a moment,

63

he seized Rajmohan's arms in an iron grasp. 'Now Bhiku,' said he to his hitherto silent companion, 'will you hold the lamp and let this fellow see my face. It is a moon face, Raju, and will please you as much as your golden moon of a wife there.' Bhiku brought the lamp and as bid held it close to his face.

'Sardar!' exclaimed Rajmohan in amazement, as he recognized his fellow-plotter of the night.

'Yes, sardar,' replied the other. 'I see you recognized me; friends never forget each other so soon.'

'What brings you here?' said he in the same angry tone as before, 'what do you want by breaking into my house?'

'First tell me,' replied the other, 'what were you going to murder your wife for.'

'That concerns you not,' returned Rajmohan. 'Leave me alone, or sardar or no sardar I will kick you out of the house.'

'Ah! Let me see your kick, prisoner as you are,' said the other sneeringly.

'My legs are free yet,' roared Rajmohan, dealing a tremendous kick at his antagonist beneath which even the sturdy frame of the robber chief staggered some paces back, involuntarily letting go his hold of the agile antagonist's arms.

'Pin him, Bhiku, pin him down,' roared the bandit as he saw Rajmohan running to regain his lost dagger; and before the sounds were uttered the vigorous arm of the second robber felled their opponent to the ground.

The sardar now sprang to the fallen man's breast with the agility and fierceness of a tiger, and while he thus held him down, the other bound Rajmohan's hands and feet with a piece of rope which, fastened to two bamboo sticks on two of the walls, had formed a sort of rude cloth-stand for Matangini.

'Now, traitor!' said the sardar. 'You are at our mercy.'

'Yes, because you are two to one—but what have I done,' asked Rajmohan, 'that you should do thus to me?'

'What have you done? You have been a traitor, know [that]! Did you not send warning to the house and save your brother-in-law? You hypocrite, you,' he added fiercely, his eyes gleaming in rage, 'you did it, you deserve to die.'

'I! I give notice to him! I would sooner tear open his eyes,' returned Rajmohan gnashing his teeth.

'Have done with your hypocrisy,' said the sardar threateningly. 'Fool that I was to believe that you would serve us against your own brother-in-law. Yet such a rascally tongue is yours, so deeply and smoothly does it lie—so often have you cursed him in our presence, that I thought I could trust you.'

'I tell you, sardar, it was not I,' returned Rajmohan with vehemence as he began to grow apprehensive for his life, for he knew well the desperate character he had to deal with. 'I tell you it was not I. Do you not remember that I left the house in your company and, till your purpose failed, have been in your company only? Have I left you for the twinkling of an eye since we went?'

'Ah! Don't hope to deceive me again; no snatching of a child's sweetmeat[1] with me. You knew your wife was awake when you brought me to your mat wall here; perhaps when you came round under the pretence of assuring yourself that she was asleep, you gave her a hint of what to do. Deny that if you can. If it was not she, can you tell me who else in the world did it?'

'*She* did it, I confess, but I can swear to you it was without my knowledge. When I came round I assure you I found her asleep. Propose the oath and I will swear that it was so.'

'You have lived long,' said the other sternly, 'it is useless now. We know you now. Do you think I would mistake the meaning of the haste with which you left as soon as the shouts from the house told us that your end had been gained? Believe me, comrade, I am too old a sinner to be deceived so easily. Prepare then to die.'

'For Heaven's sake descend from my bosom,' said Rajmohan, gasping for breath. The heavy burden of the bandit's body was pressing on his chest and at length became unsupportable even to his strength and iron frame. 'Release me. I swear to you by my patron God it was not so. I swear to you by my mother I did not know it.'

'How did your wife do it then?' enquired the bandit chief in the same tone as before.

With this question he alighted from the breast of the other, but kept a hold on his throat by a light grasp prepared to tighten at the least hostile movement from his prisoner.

'Could it not be,' said Rajmohan, now breathing free, 'that she had only counterfeited sleep when I saw her?'

'Ha! Ha! You take me for a fool,' said the sardar with a gurgling laugh. 'I wanted to stand off from the wall, you made me come to the wall; why was that? Why, but for this treachery? You have betrayed us to Madhav Ghose; who can say you will [not] betray [us] to the police also, for that man will protect you? You must die or there is no safety for [us. You] gave us the slip very smartly or you would not live till now.'

'And what?' exclaimed Rajmohan with a sudden vehemence, 'What did you see when you came in? Was I not going to murder the very woman whom [you] say I employed as my agent? But for your interference [she] would have been a corpse now.'

'*Han*,' exclaimed the sardar in an altered [voice, as he]

gazed steadily on his silent comrade as if [to ask] what he thought of the [matter.]

'Yes, sardar, he speaks truth,' said Bhiku, [breaking] silence for the first time. 'Why else should he [kill] the woman.'

'I was going to kill her,' said Rajmohan with a shudder, 'for having done the very deed you charge me with.'

'The woman! The woman! Kill the woman,' said the sardar as he sprang to the spot where he had seen Rajmohan's wife sink at her husband's uplifted blade.

He alighted on a heap of clothes which he had mistaken for his intended victim in the dim light of the expiring lamp.

'Wretch,' muttered he, 'you need not escape me—don't think a sardar can't hunt you out in this little room.'

'Stop,' said Rajmohan, recovering the accustomed energy of his voice. 'None but myself touches my wife; unbind me.'

'Unbind him, Bhiku, while I drag her out by her hair,' said the sardar as he jumped to another corner where he saw something white again. Bhiku quickly cut Rajmohan's bandages with his sword. '*Het!* Clothes again!' muttered the robber as again he struck the hilt of his sword at a cane *petara*. 'But! out! Wicked woman,' said he highly exasperated and struck his weapon here and there on the bedstead. There was no Matangini on the bedstead.

'Here, Bhiku, bring the lamp here,' roared the sardar once more, 'the woman has hid herself beneath the taktaposh.' Bhiku brought the lamp, trimming it well. Rajmohan followed; all then bent down to look beneath the taktaposh for the affrighted fugitive, when lo! nobody was there.

Lifting the lamp high they could see by its improved light every corner and angle of the room, but Matangini was nowhere.

'The door! The door!' exclaimed Rajmohan, 'Look! It is unbarred. I had barred it when I entered. She has fled.'

Matangini had indeed fled. Profiting by the mutual quarrel [of the robbers who] were too deeply engaged in their own [life] and death struggle to remember her whom less brutal hearts could never forget, Matangini had stolen away unperceived to the door, which she had quietly unbarred, and it is to be doubted if far more clamorous proceedings on her part would have attracted the attention of combatants so busily engaged.

'Run, run after her,' said the sardar. 'She will ruin us.'

'Yes, run,' said Rajmohan. 'But hark you, none but I lift a finger against my wife. I will kill her when she is found, or if I do not, kill me as you proposed. But no one else must touch her. Haste, I will precede you.'

The three rushed out. The skies were still murky and continued drizzling. The fair fugitive was searched for in every direction. Day was now dawning fast, and little time was left for the search.

Rajmohan's first thought was to peep at Kanak's house. He and the sardar stealthily approached the hut and ascending to the level of the floor, slightly removed the jhamp which closed it. There they beheld in the faint grey light admitted by the opening thus made the sleeping forms of mother and daughter only. They looked over the neighbouring bushes, but with the same ill-success. A bright and ruddy morning was now following the wet and murky dawn too fast to render the search safe for the dacoits any longer. They then separated for the present, appointing a place of rendezvous at night, the sardar [uttering] an obscene threat to [ensure the) attendance of the suspected Rajmohan.

The Friends and the Stranger

THE RECENT SHOWER HAD LENT TO THE MORNING A DELIGHTFUL and invigorating freshness. Leaving the mass of floating clouds behind, the sun advanced and careered on the vast blue plain that shone above; and every housetop and every treetop, the cocoa palm and the date palm, the mango and the acacia received the flood of splendid light and rejoiced. The still-lingering water drops on the leaves of trees and creepers glittered and shone like a thousand radiant gems as they received the slanting rays of the luminary. Through the openings in the chick-knit boughs of the groves glanced the mild ray on the moistened grass beneath. The newly awakened and joyous birds raised their thousand dissonant voices, while at intervals the papia sent forth its rich thrilling notes into the trembling air. Light fleecy clouds of white wandered in the solitude of the now purified blue of the heavens, which were fanned by a light breeze that had sprung up to shake the pattering drops from the pendant and wooing boughs.

The reader will now follow us to the pool which had been the scene of Matangini's temporary danger and escape on the previous night. The sun had run a two hours' course in the heavens. Beneath a young tamarind tree, where the surrounding underwood lent a sort of cover, Matangini sat on the moist grass. Her clothes were wet; her sari had been soiled by mud, her usually curly tresses, washed by the drizzling rain, now fell in straight and loosely flowing bands on her neck and arms; and her head was slightly bent to permit the sunbeams to play on that raven hair, darker than any cloud which had ever opposed their progress through the atmosphere. Close by her was to be seen the rather full and developed figure of Kanak shining with recently rubbed oil. A dirty napkin thrown over her neck, the brass *kalsi* maintaining its capacious but as yet empty bulk close by its mistress, and the blue *mishi* which had recently been called upon to lend its hue to her teeth, showed that the morning ablutions had drawn Kanak out of her home, but that important business had not been hitherto performed. The friends were evidently engaged in an earnest and interesting conversation. The reader need not be informed that with much of the subject of this interesting dialogue, he is already acquainted. Matangini was pouring cautiously and in whispers a narrative of the occurrences of the eventful night into the faithful and discreet ears of her only friend. The concluding part of this conversation we shall, with the reader's leave, place before him for his gratification.

'*Ma gow!*'[1] said Kanak with a shudder, after having listened for some time in silent and mute astonishment. 'Ah! Were it I, I would have been dead through fear. But you are a brave woman. But do you think of returning to your husband's house?'

'Where else can I go?' replied Matangini with a deep drawn sigh.

'Ah, do not, do not return, I beseech you,' returned Kanak vehemently, 'they will kill you.'

'I know my death is inevitable, but who can help fate? Who will tell me how I can find a shelter elsewhere?' and Matangini wept.

'My house will be no shelter for you, I know well,' replied Kanak, her eyes brimming over with tears in sympathy for the affliction of her friend. 'But you must not return home. Why will you not go to your sister?'

Matangini's features changed; she dashed the tear drops from her eyes, and assuming the same energy of voice in which she had bidden Madhav farewell, said, 'Never! Never again while life lasts.'

Matangini's manner silenced all contradiction. Kanak covered her face with her anchal and wept.

'Ah, mothers!' interrupted a voice from behind 'What are you speaking of in secret? Ah, you are weeping I see; why, what is the matter?'

The new speaker who stood by the startled friends, was a middle-aged woman of a dark complexion. Her hair had turned partly grey and her countenance was fast becoming wrinkled. She was dressed in a coarse *thenthe*, rather clean; her freshly oiled face, the dirty napkin on her shoulder, as well as the empty kalsi on her waist, betokened the nature of her visit to the waterside.

'Why, it is Suki's mother,' said Kanak, forgetting her tears and laughing and smiling in an instant. 'Why, Suki's mother, why this unusual visit to the Phulpukur[2] today?'

'I rose late this morning,' replied Suki's mother with benignant civility, 'and so, hasty of going to work direct, I thought of washing myself first. But what has happened, child? Why are you both weeping?'

'Ah, Suki's mother!' said Kanak, her eyes again moistening. 'How shall I speak of this poor woman's misfortunes?' A quiet but significant glance from Matangini's eye, which meant that her misfortunes were such as should not meet strangers' ears, warned Kanak against indiscreet disclosures; but Kanak, replying by a glance as full of meaning, seemed to imply that her secrets were safe.

'Talk not of her misfortunes,' said Kanak to the newcomer.

'The wretched woman has been turned out of her house by her husband and she knows not where to seek a shelter.'

'Oh fie,' exclaimed Suki's mother, 'is that a thing to weep for? Husbands and wives quarrel in the morning and become reconciled in the evening—who does not know that! He is angry now—he will entreat you to go home as soon as his anger is gone. Fie, mother, why do you weep for that? Ah, Kanak, when my son-in-law comes to see us, there is not a night when he does not quarrel with my daughter. But what of that? He loves my daughter as no one else loves his wife. Even last Wednesday, he came and brought her a handsome gold *noth*—and such a noth, Kanak!' Kanak cut short the happy mother's description of her son-in-law's amiable disposition by observing, 'True, Suki's mother, but Raju-da³ wants to marry another girl—the match that came from Junglebariah; you know well now why he treats her after this fashion, often and often; she will not go home again, Suki's mother, no woman ought to go. She will never trust herself again to that house to receive insults and reproaches. But alas, poor woman, whither else can she go! Is her father's hut close by to give her shelter?'

'Ah, what a hard fate!' said the good dame, sympathizing, 'No no, if she be worthy of the name of woman, she cannot return home. Marry again! Why, where could he get a more beautiful wife? And will the little child he will bring home be a housewife like her? No, mother, do not return but go to your sister and see what he will do.'

'Alas! Suki's mother, she cannot go to her sister even,' responded Kanak, Matangini silently eyeing the ground from shame and confusion. 'She has quarrelled with her sister because Madhav Babu did not invite her husband at the late *shradh*. I could indeed give her shelter, but we are poor, Suki's mother, and I cannot take her there to starve.'

'My death; but what a simple-hearted woman is she,' replied Suki's mother. 'She quarrelled with her sister on behalf of such a husband! The man does not deserve such a wife. Were he my son-in-law, I would have scolded not only him but his mother and his father too; but come, mother,' said she, turning to the silent and confused Matangini, 'come with me and live with my mistress as long as you choose; the elder Thakurani likes you so much that she will be overjoyed to see you. There, when your husband forgets his anger, and entreats you to go,—for soon he will—you can return to your own house. But do not listen to him too soon; first see that tears flow from his eyes—and that he takes the straw between his teeth.'[4]

'Ah! Yes, yes!' exclaimed Kanak joyfully. 'You have spoken well, Suki's mother. She will go with you now; what say you, sister? Will it not be the best thing to go with Suki's mother? The elder Thakurani, I am sure, loves you; you must be quite welcome to her. Why do you not speak?' Matangini frowned, but without heeding her, her loquacious friend went on glibly. 'Yes, yes, she will go; go, bathe yourself, Suki's mother, and when you return she will follow you. Go then, delay not.'

Suki's mother hastened to perform her morning ablutions. When the friends were alone, Matangini spoke. 'To what a depth am I fallen, Kanak!' said she.

Kanak returned with an impressive energy of manner, 'Oh! Do not say nay—drink my blood if you do.[5] Go—go now; in the evening I will see you—be silent.'

Kanak waited not for a reply, but taking her kalsi up in haste, she ran to the waterside to join Suki's mother and to perform her morning ablutions.

The Protectress

THE HOUSE OF MATHUR GHOSE[1] WAS A GENUINE SPECIMEN OF mofussil magnificence united with mofussil want of cleanliness.

From the far-off paddy fields you could descry through the intervening foliage, its high palisades and blackened walls. On a nearer view might be seen pieces of plaster of venerable antiquity prepared to bid farewell to their old and weather-beaten tenement. Some rude and unpainted shutter hanging by a single hinge whose companion had left the precincts years before, while in others both hinge and plank had left little trace of their existence and had been supplanted by the less pretentious tribe of *tat* screens. But a small portion of the huge edifice had ever been plastered on the outside. On the favoured region which boasted such decoration, and which no doubt composed the sanctum sanctorum of some great man in the house, if not Mathur Ghose himself, you might descry a few apologies for venetians, but window panes the giant house had eschewed as too frail a substance to be permitted to ornament its limbs. By far the greater part of the exterior was unplastered, and the dried slime and soot reposed on the mass of bricks in murky grandeur. Not unfrequently a young shoot of a bur or a less noble vegetable had struck its roots in the crevices between the layers of brick, realizing, rather on an humble scale, the Persian monarch's dream of a hanging garden.

The house was divided into four distinct sections. In front you entered through a pair of massive iron-plated and tar-coloured doors into a spacious courtyard, three sides of which

were faced by double-storeyed verandas of no very respectable
height. Opposite the portal arose the lofty and spacious hall
of five arches. All around was well plastered, but the return of
many a rainy season had variegated the white with streaks
of dark, particularly in those regions which were surmounted
by spouts for drawing off the water from the top. A mazy suite
of dark and damp apartments led from a corner of this part of
the building to the inner *mahal*, another quadrangle, on all
four sides of which towered double-storeyed verandas as
before. These had indeed a plastering of sand and lime, but few
were the pillars which wore these decorations entire, decay
aided by the manipulations of idle children having stripped
most of them of their coverings. The walls of all the chambers
above and below were well striped with numerous streaks of
red, white, black, green, all colours of the rainbow, caused by
the spittles of such as had found their mouths too much
encumbered with paan or by some improvident woman servant
who had broken the *golahandi* while it was full of its muddy
contents, most frequently by the fingers of her whose pleasant
task it had been to prepare the betel leaves, and who had
cleverly impressed the walls into her service and had made
them act as substitutes for towels. Numerous sketches in
charcoal, which showed, we fear, nothing of the conception of
Angelo or the tinting of Guido,[2] attested the art or idleness
of the wicked boys and ingenious girls who had contrived
to while away hungry hours by essays in the arts of designing
and of defacing wall. The courtyard, devoid of brick or tile,
exposed mother earth in all her vegetable glories. The said
vegetable glories, however, were gathered at the four corners
leaving in the centre paths in several directions for entrance
and exit. Household filth and water had left thick crusts of

slime which reposed for ages in unmitigated blackness. A narrow passage, terminated by a small thick door, led you to the third section of the house. This was the kitchen of the household; it had two suites of one-storeyed apartments on two sides of a vast courtyard where vegetation was much more rank than in the other. Here might be always seen the traces of the havoc daily made on vegetables of the earth, and the fishes of the water by the good dames in charge of this useful department,[3] and here too might be seen the empire of soot in all the majesty of darkness. The fourth department lay behind the kitchen, but apparently all access to it was barred from this side and few were the females of the household who had ever set their feet on it.

A thick and massive door led to the 'godown' as the mahal was called by the males, directly from outside. Bare but high walls, the summits of which were secured against the invasion of human feet by broken fragments of bottles, enclosed it on three sides. On the fourth stood the single row of one-storeyed apartments which it contained. The walls of the apartments were all of unusual thickness, the doors small and plated with iron, and not a window was to be seen. The use to which these 'godowns' were put was known to be that of storehouses for all sorts of things. A vast garden of *supari*[4] trees interspersed with *bakul*, stood on one side of the building, and being enclosed on all sides by brick walls and containing a well-filled tank in the middle, composed the khirki[5] of the household. The passage to it lay through the precincts of the cook, from which a small door opened on the garden.

The reader will be good enough to ascend in our company, through a flight of dark and narrow stairs of solid brickwork to the upper storey of the andarmahal, properly so called, that which formed the second section of the large edifice a view of which we have placed before him. We invite him to enter a no less unapproached and unapproachable region than the bedchamber of Mathur Ghose himself. The polished plastering of the walls was clean enough, though not unfrequently could stains and scratches be seen defacing its purity. A little towards one end of the room stood a massive and high cot of teakwood on the uncovered floor over which loosely hung a striped gauze curtain, rather disproportioned to the wooden frame. A few huge almirahs and chests of drawers of the same material, the varnish of which had considerably been soiled by time and rough usage, lined the foot of the walls opposite to the cot. One or two escritoires, as well as some common country boxes and chests decorated with enormous brass plates across their lids and on the edges, and ornamented with semilunes of *chandan*, completed the wooden furniture of the room. Two paintings of the largest size, from one of which glowered the grim black figure of Kali, and on the other of which was displayed the crab-like form of Durga,[6] faced each other from high position on two opposite walls.

On the two remaining walls, and placed lower than the terrific Kali and the gorgeous Durga, might be seen arrayed a few specimens of European art, and the exquisite conception of the Virgin and Child[7] might itself be seen adorning the chamber the inmates of which had little knowledge what the artist's genius and engraver's skill had strove to represent. A female of about twenty-eight years of age sat on a windowsill. Her face and figure were still handsome. Her complexion was that of a brunette[8] and her eyes were large, dark, and shone with a mild and almost benignant lustre. Beyond this there was nothing particularly remarkable in her countenance, unless it was the expression of sweetness and amiability that never abandoned it. A clean sari covered her rounded limbs and frame, but not her head, which was now uncovered; and the crisp and shining tresses of hair, rendered still more so by recent ablution, fell loosened on the back, scattered and uncombed, but still beautiful from their irregular luxuriance. Golden ornaments of great value but rather of lighter make than usual, graced her ears, her neck, her bosom and arms and wrists. For some reason or other the fine and delicate circumference of the noth was absent from her nostril and cheek, but the tinkling malls maintained their place in her ankles. A few long ringlets of human hair tied to the window grating furnished occupation to her little fingers as she tried to weave them into that oft-coveted object of young girls, the hair string. A child of about ten years in whose exquisitely handsome features might be discerned a likeness to the elder female, sat by her and proved by the interest she took in the occupation of the latter that it was to tie in bondage her own wild locks that the product of her mother's delicate labours was destined. A little removed from them, modest, confused, melancholy, sat another woman who, however, needs no introduction. Suki's mother—the mother-in-law of whose felicity the reader has had her own description—had redeemed her promise by leading the reluctant Matangini to the presence of Mathur's first or eldest wife—the female who was weaving the hair strings for her daughter.

A dialogue was being carried on between Mathur's wife and Matangini in a low voice, while Suki's mother was pouring on a loose prattle without any apprehensions of interrupting either. We need not detain the reader with a detail of either the dialogue or the prattle, as of their purport we will do him the justice to presume he has already some conception. Suki's mother had rendered her mistress acquainted with the unfortunate position of the refugee, so far as she had gathered them from the rather unfaithful version of Kanak, embellishing the narrative with a good many interpolations of her own, and a few observations on connubial felicity as exemplified by the lot of her own happy daughter. The good dame rightly judged that such embellishments and interpolations would do no harm to the interests of her protégée; while at the same time they would afford a varied field for the display of her own powers of harangue. Matangini had not the heart to disclose the real circumstances of her misfortune, especially in the presence of the servant. She therefore unwillingly passed over most points in the good woman's narrative in silence, intending to undeceive her new friend, should it be necessary for her to trespass long on her kindness, on a future occasion, and with so much reserve as might be necessary to conceal the depth to which her husband had fallen. Mathur's wife gave her the warmest and most cordial welcome, rendering it apparent by an intuitive generosity of heart wholly dissimilar to acquired polish of manners, that she rather pressed an invitation than afforded shelter. One step, however, was indispensable before Matangini could be enrolled a member of the household; Mathur Ghose's permission had to be obtained. With the intention of requesting it, she deputed the still eloquent parent of the happy daughter to the *sadar*[9] to request her husband to step inside for a moment, without, however, mentioning her object before Matangini. After a few minutes, her husband entered the chamber, the wife drew her cloth over her head, and Matangini, as etiquette required, stepped out, not, however, without meeting a fixed gaze of recognition and wonder from the eyes of the master of the house.

Between Rival Charmers

Containing a dissension on connubial warfare.——A siege and a dubious capitulation.

MATHUR GHOSE, AS OUR READER HAD NO DOUBT GUESSED IN THE course of the previous chapter, had the good fortune or misfortune of being blessed or incommoded by double ties of matrimony and was the master or slave or both of [his] two wives. Tara, the elder, has already been introduced; Champak, the younger, was Tara's junior by not less than eight years. She possessed decided superiority over her rival in the regularity of her features and in the blooming fairness of her complexion. To this, nature had added a witchery of coquettish grace that marked the movements of this proud and insolent beauty which won for her the envied distinction of the proudest damsel in the vicinity. Proud and imperious, Champak ever ruled the household with the authority of its sole mistress. The household approached her with fear and perhaps with a secret feeling of dislike, for often it was that her naughty temper made them feel that every fair face is not the reflector of a generous heart. And, in spite of the rival and superior claims of Tara, she was the real as well as the apparent mistress of the house. Mathur Ghose was not perhaps formed by nature to love and be loved; affection was not certainly the ruling passion of his heart, but the power of woman and her beauty have their influence upon all, and Mathur Ghose was fond of his wife. Sensibility and refinement of the heart lend to the passion of love the form of a fervent and etherialized feeling which finds its gratification in the communings of heart with heart; while, in grosser natures, it degenerates into the yearnings of desire or perhaps into a blind obedience to the mystic power of female loveliness; but the strength of the passion can be equally great in either case. It was not strange therefore that Mathur loved Champak, or if we may not use the word love, was fond of her blindly and ardently. The master who bent with an iron will the interest of all who surrounded him to subserve his own—was but a slave to the will of this coquette. To Tara, whose sweetness and patience put it beyond his power to be offended—he was indifferent, too much so perhaps to be ever unkind.

Tara had procured an easy assent from her husband to her proposal that the wife of Rajmohan should find a shelter in their house. 'Food and clothing,' Mathur said in reply, 'are not scarce in my house, under the blessing of the gods and the Brahmans, and if the woman is as you say of good character, let her remain here as long as she chooses.' But Tara's simple heart had not reckoned upon an opposition which certainly was powerful enough to counteract her benevolence. Champak liked not that it should be under the auspices of her rival that the stranger should obtain a footing in the household.

The sun was shedding its mellowed parting beams on the house of Mathur Ghose, and the day which had been ushered in amidst the gloomy deeds which threatened the fate of Matangini was hastening to a close. The slanting rays fell at intervals on an open veranda, on the second floor. Tara was seated on the bare ground and was employed in tying the hair of her daughter into a *khompa*,[1] the knots and bends of which however satisfied neither herself nor the child. Matangini sat close by answering with reserve to some very provoking and impertinent questions, while Champak, employed in painting her little feet with the lac dye, by the aid of a barber's garrulous wife, was pouring upon her, without the consciousness that a refugee to whom her husband had afforded shelter from mere compassion and whom she herself could turn out any moment, could ever entertain reluctance to answer questions coming from herself direct. Matangini was answering with meekness and reserve, which, however, had merely the effect of provoking further impertinence from the haughty beauty. Tara saw the vexation of her protégée, and delicately interfered by drawing off the attention of both.

'I can't tie this child's khompa, though you see I have been trying my hand at it since noon,' said she addressing Matangini. 'You can do it better perhaps. If you will only show me, how to turn this *binuni*, I think I can do the rest.' Matangini asked to be permitted to tie the braids for the day herself.

'I do not think I can do it well,' she said, 'but I will do what I can.'

Matangini took her position behind the child and taking up the braids in her hands, began to untie them and form new ones.

'Aha!' said Champak, 'I fear our sister will make only one of her western country khompas. It is best as it is.'

'If I succeed in tying a khompa as they do in our part of the country,'[2] returned Matangini, 'this beautiful child will look twice more beautiful.'

'No, no—you must not do it,' rejoined Champak, 'that is the way in which disreputable females dress their hair—it does not look seemly in good people's children.'

'O fie!' interposed Tara. 'Is beauty ever disdained because sometimes a bad woman is beautiful? At that rate, sister, you should have disfigured your own fine countenance long before this. No, no, because bad women may have a fine knot of hair, that is no reason why a good woman should have none. Tie the knot as you please, sister,' concluded she, addressing Matangini.

Champak replied not, but it was evident from the sullen looks she assumed that Tara's compliment had not been enough to make her forget that she was refused her own way. The tread of heavy slipshod feet was just then heard downstairs, and Mathur Ghose soon appeared in the veranda. Champak drew her cloth over her face down to the very chin and lightly tripped to her own chamber, her malls tinkling as she ran; Tara drew her cloth over her face also but not to the same depth, and slowly rose to retire; Matangini covered herself also, and stood aside. Mathur Ghose stopped to speak with his daughter to whom he addressed a few ordinary questions. Champak who was watching him from behind the door observed, and jealous wife as she was, observed it with dismay, that though he addressed the child alone his eyes occasionally wandered with an eager glance towards the veiled form of the stranger. Mathur Ghose passed on to the apartment of his younger wife, and the interrupted females resumed their occupations with the exception of Champak whom her husband found in the apartment.

Champak well knew that the steps of her husband would seek her there, and she herself sought an interview. But to avoid the appearance of having sought her room in the expectation of meeting him, she hastily opened a box as soon as she saw him leave the veranda, and busied herself in taking out of it some choice spices used in preparing the betel leaf for mastication. Mathur Ghose saw the floor strewed[3] with many a silver, horn, or wooden *kauta*[4] without end or aim, and his wife little inclined to take any notice of his entrance. Her face was still partly covered with her cloth, her back was turned towards her husband and the work of strewing the floor with little boxes of cardamoms, cinnamon, cloves, almonds, went on bravely progressing. After waiting for a few moments in silence, Mathur observed, 'What is the matter now? Some storm brewing I suppose?'

Champak answered not, but went on strewing the floor with kautas after kautas.

'Aha, I see it,' said Mathur, 'now tell me for what offence I have to pay the penalty.'

But still Champak did not reply. She now began to gather up the kautas as if she had found what she sought, and having replaced them in the box and locked them up she turned towards the door to go out.

'That won't do, my life!' said Mathur as he arrested her progress by catching her by the arm. 'This cursed *ghomta* has no business here,' and he pushed back the cloth from her face.

'Why do you detain me?' asked Champak, casting on him a look of high displeasure.

'Tell me, my life, what have I done that you wear this look?'

'Let me go,' she said, though of course no entreaty was needed to obtain her release as her husband held her arm by a light and loving grasp, and she could have had her pleasure if only she were so minded, 'let me go, I have business.'

'You have business, my lily-face? What can this business be?' enquired Mathur, laughing.

'I have to prepare paan,' responded she with the same irritable look

'Do it then here and let me have some,' said he.

'Let me go,' said she again.

'Why, what is [it]?' said Mathur fondly. 'Name but my offence to you and I promise you expiation.'

'Offence to me,' said she in the same pettish manner, 'what offence can you be guilty of towards me? What am I that I can be offended with you? You can do what you please without offending anybody——and I am nobody.'

'*Sabash*,' said he, 'this is anger indeed! But tell me, queen of [my] life, what it is that I must undo, and I will undo it immediately.'

'Go to the wife you love,' she said, 'and she may tell you if there is anything to undo, and undo it then.——What matter to you the wishes of a poor woman who no further trespasses on your bounty than to live in your household which even strangers are permitted to do?'

'Oh! Can it be *that*?' asked Mathur, now comprehending how matters stood——'Are you angry that I have taken the poor woman to my household at the'——he would have added——'at the intercession of your rival,'——but he forbore and stopped short,

'It is your house,' returned she, still with apparent displeasure, but now glad at heart that he had divined the cause of her displeasure, 'you can admit anybody you please.'

'But seriously,' he added with earnestness of manner, 'let go womanishness now and tell me truly how you can object to my affording temporary shelter to such a forlorn creature.'

'Forlorn creature!' returned Champak. 'Why, if she has done ill, she has deserved to be turned out.'

'And how do you know she has done ill?'

'Why, do you think she would be turned out for nothing? Do people turn out their wives from caprice?'

'Yes—it may be she was wrong—it may also be her husband was wrong. But still it cannot be wrong to give her shelter in the house in any case.'

'You can do your pleasure,' she returned sulkily again. 'Why do you ask my opinion about it at all?'

'There again! Fie, a woman should be more kind.'

'Yes, kind to those who deserve kindness. But is it right to be kind to all alike, be she good or bad?'

'But still you cannot be sure she has not been more unfortunate than anything else, and report speaks very favourably of her conduct.'

'Report!' said Champak with a contemptuous swing of her large fine noth. 'You have picked up all your information on the point from Suki's mother's little gossip and you dignify her garrulous lies with the name of *report*.'

'Why, have you heard anyone speak otherwise than well of her?' enquired Mathur rather surprised.

'Women always hear more of each other than men,' said she.

'What have you heard?' Mathur again enquired.

'What propriety is this in you,' replied she a little archly now, 'to enquire about the secrets of women?'

Mathur Ghose felt vexed. From whatever motives, he evidently desired that Matangini should enjoy the benefit of his protection, and he felt vexed, as we have said, at this unexpected resistance from one who, he was aware, was pretty well accustomed to have her own will.

'At least you will admit,' he added after musing for some time, 'you will admit that it looks very bad to turn out a kinswoman from the house, for you know she is a kinswoman of ours. Has she not a claim upon us?'

'She is our kinswoman through another kinswoman,' was the ready reply. 'Why has she not sought shelter with her sister? Are we nearer or dearer to her than her sister? She dares not perhaps to seek shelter with those who know her well.'

'You are very ungenerous,' returned Mathur in vexation of spirit. 'What can you have to object to in an unfriended woman? Is there want of food or raiment in my house?'

'No,' returned she proudly, 'at least I shall not claim my share if she become welcome to them. Send me to my father's house and let her live here. My father is not one who will be pleased to see his daughter the inmate of a house in which such a woman lives.'

'What is all this again?' Mathur said, becoming irritated.

'Send me to my father's house,' she replied.

'You know I cannot part with you. Leave off childishness,' returned he, softening.

'Then part with that woman,' was the reply.

'Part with the woman; why, what is she to me that there is any difficulty in my parting with her? Well, I will think of it.'

With these words Mathur left the room, resolved to prevaricate and deceive his wife till her mind should change.

That evening when he again returned to the chamber, an extraordinary spectacle presented itself to his eyes. In a corner of the room, far apart from his bedstead, another bed had been neatly prepared on a humble couch which had been pitched up from the room for service.

'What is that for?' asked Mathur, as the additional bed caught his eye. Champak spoke not, but throwing herself on it, went to sleep without deigning a reply.

Our readers will guess what a night the uxorious Mathur Ghose passed. When he rose next morning and went out to his *baithak-khana*, he observed a visitor waiting for him, who said he was Rajmohan Ghose. He explained to Mathur the object of his visit to be that, having obtained intelligence that his wife who had left his house on pretence of a quarrel was here, he had come over to request that she be made [to] return. Mathur could not well refuse to restore a wife to her husband, a course which, he had been taught, was become[5] necessary to him to pursue on other considerations, if he had any relish for domestic peace and the smiles of Champak.

When Matangini was informed that she must depart, her blood froze within her as she reflected on the fate that awaited her. More dead than alive, she followed the steps of Suki's mother, who was entrusted with the duty of escorting her home. Tara accompanied her as far as the postern gate and would gladly have gone further if she could. She bade her farewell with sorrow and heartily wished her peace and oblivion of past disagreements with her husband.

Consultations and Council

THE WILD AND LOVELY SHORES OF THE MADHUMATI ARE COVERED even in the vicinity of well-inhabited villages by a tall rank grass almost impervious to human feet. Such a spot of peculiar and almost frightful solitude lay a little to the south of Radhaganj. There the impervious grass was intermixed with an equally high and impervious range of cane bushes and other underwood which extended far into the land from the margin of the river. Were there a site in the vicinity which commanded an unbroken view of the whole area covered by the interminable underwood, not a single interruption could have been discerned to its luxuriant uniformity. One narrow footpath seemed to present the only evidence that human footsteps had ever disturbed this dark habitation of venomous reptiles. But even this footpath could be discerned upon the closest observation and for a short distance only, and then every trace of its further progress was lost. To the practised eye of those, however, who were wont to thread its maze, it presented the only guidance to a little hovel of straw which stood in the very heart of the jungle. The roof of the hovel, a little elevated above the general height of the bushes, was carefully concealed from the view of curious eyes outside by so drawing off and arranging the twigs of adjacent boughs that the whole thatch wore the appearance of the top of a bush higher than the rest. The inside of this small and wretched habitation, if such it could be called, was gloomy and damp. The walls were of bamboo and *darma*, and two or three

darmas were spread over the humid floor. Blackened pots
and cooking utensils were stowed in one corner of the hovel,
though apparently they were not often put to use. It was still
early in the morning and the streaks of sunbeams that had
penetrated inside through crevices had the length that [slanting]
rays alone could possess. Its only inhabitants [were] men of a
deep black complexion and of a stature and muscular formation
that promised vast strength. A short and coarse cloth of
small width lightly covered the waist of each, but their legs and
thighs and the rest of their dark bodies were completely naked.
Latties and swords lay scattered beside them and betokened
that their profession was anything but peaceful. The noxious
fume of ganja which was being smoked by the two by turns,
filled the whole cabin. They were engaged in conversing
with each other in a guarded tone which the secluded locality
made little necessary.

'What will the business bring?' asked one in whom the
reader will recognize Bhiku.

'A large sum,' responded his companion who was no other
than the sardar, 'full five thousand rupees. It is as good as a
night's affair; nay better, for we go shares with nobody.'

'Bosh!' ejaculated Bhiku, his dull eyes glistening with joy.
'But why will you not attempt it on the road when that lawyer
carries it with him? How else can you get hold of it elsewhere?'

'Because you know that accursed wench, Rajmohan's wife,
had overheard me talking to her husband about it,' replied the
sardar, 'and has informed Madhav that we wanted it. He has
warning and means to send the paper under good escort. And
we are only two. Do you now understand, you monkey?'

'But how can we get at it otherwise?' observed the other.
'Two of us cannot force the house.'

'Leave that to me, leave that to me. Wit will succeed where strength fails.'

Bhiku pulled a long puff at his chillum and then leisurely sent out the smoke in curls before him. Then shaking his head he observed, 'No, no, sardar, I don't see how it can be done. I tell you one thing, will not our employer advance us one of the five thousands he has promised? It will be a more profitable business then; he cannot find us out when we leave this place.'

'Do you think him such a fool?' replied the sardar. 'Do hear what conditions the sharp bargainer has proposed. He gives us one thousand when we can show him the paper to be in our possession; we receive three thousands in all when we deliver it to his hands. And only when the suit is won, which will surely be if the will is destroyed, will we get the other two thousands.'

'But, then, tell me how we are to rob it.'

'No, no, no! You will spoil the business if you know it beforehand. Cunning Rajmohan may make you give it out to him. Follow me as my shadow and rest assured we will succeed.'

'Rajmohan cheat me that way!' exclaimed Bhiku with some enthusiasm, but immediately lowering his voice he said, 'Hush I hear footsteps approaching.'

A cry like that of screech-owls but evidently uttered in a human voice, was heard from within the jungle.

'It is only Rajmohan,' observed the sardar and responded by a similar cry. Rajmohan soon made his appearance at the hovel.

'What news, Raj?' asked the sardar.

'All is well,' replied Rajmohan, 'I have got back my wife.'

'Indeed! How was it? Where was she?' asked he with some show of satisfaction.

'Well it is rather strange,' said Rajmohan. 'Instead of going to her sister where did she go, think you?'

'Where?' enquired both the banditti.

'Why, did not I think she would go there? The house of Mathur Ghose himself.'

'Indeed, and what has she been saying?'

'I believe, nothing, so far as I could gather. I had some talk with the domestics on purpose, but I believe they had no suspicion of anything.'

'Still,' said the sardar, lowering his eyes while a fierce glance shot therefrom, 'we must get rid of her.'

'Why, consider,' said Rajmohan, 'consider if she may not be spared.'

'Ah! Was I right when I said you were—'

'Hear me sardar, hear me out,' interrupted Rajmohan with vehemence. 'I hate that wretched woman more than you can ever do. Had I found her out that morning, you would have seen I am no lover. But I confess now that my blood has cooled, I have not the courage and cruelty to do such a deed. Besides, what we feared she had not done; she neither went to Madhav Ghose's house, nor made a noise of last night's affair. If she has not done it today, what reason is there that she will do it tomorrow.'

'Well,' said the sardar, musing, 'I have a place and it may suit both your mind and ours.'

'What is it?' enquired Rajmohan.

'Pack up, take your beautiful wife with you, and come and live with us at Mitguntie.'

'And lead the life of a robber?'

'Yes. Are you not one?'

'Perhaps, but it is impossible for me to be one by reputation.'

'You decline to go?'

'Yes, I have others to take care of, besides this wretched wife. Can I lead the ilk of a robber with such a family?'

'Have we not our families there?'

'Yes—but then mine must not know that they live with—'

'Peace!' exclaimed the sardar, interrupting him authoritatively. 'If you want to join us you can easily send off your sister and her children to her husband,—poor husband or rich husband, it is no lookout of yours; and as to your aunt, she is the aunt of many others like yourself and can shift for herself.'

Rajmohan still hesitated. A long debate ensued, but the threats of the sardar joined to his own wish to leave the neighbourhood of Madhav Ghose forever, at length prevailed on Rajmohan, and he consented.

It was yet wanting to noon when Rajmohan returned home to bathe himself and break his fast.

The first person who met his eyes was his sister Kishori.

'Kishori,' he said to her, 'tell the wretched woman to come before me. I shall teach her how to run away again from my house.'

'Whom do you mean, brother?' enquired Kishori.

'Whom? Why, your sister-in-law,' exclaimed Rajmohan, irritated at the question. 'Where can your senses be gone?'

'My sister-in-law is not here, you know,' replied Kishori.

'Not here!' ejaculated Rajmohan in surprise. 'Has she not returned in the morning?'

'You said you would send her here from the "Elder House",' returned Kishori, 'but you have not done so.'

Rajmohan started up in anger and surprise. 'It is false!' he cried. 'I myself saw her coming in that woman Suki's mother's company.'

'That's strange,' replied Kishori, 'but she has not returned. Ask anybody here—none has seen her.' Rajmohan flew like a tiger round the house and ransacked every part of it, but could not find Matangini skulking anywhere.

'Run,' he cried to his sister, 'run to her sister's house; the wretch has sheltered herself there no doubt. Stop—ask aunt to go over to Kanak's house and look for her there. She may be there. I shall keep watch for her here.'

Both Kishori and her aunt started on their errands, but both returned unsuccessfully. Vexation, rage, and surprise bewildered the disappointed husband. With angry words and gestures he again compelled his sister to undertake another fatiguing journey in the midday to learn by enquiry in Mathur Ghose's household if Matangini had not returned. The obedient Kishori executed her commission with patience and fidelity, but could not succeed in bringing any news of her sister-in-law.

What Befell Our Hero

THREE DAYS HAD ELAPSED SINCE THE OCCURRENCES OF the last chapter. The night was dark, and the brilliant and trembling light in Madhav's room, which could be seen from afar, showed in rich contrast with the impenetrable gloom beyond. Madhav Ghose was alone, He sat reclining on a mahogany couch covered with satin. A single but well-fed light illumined the chamber. Some two or three English books were scattered over the couch, and one of these Madhav held in his hand but he hardly read it. He sat with his abstracted gaze fixed on the dark but star-besprinkled heavens which were visible through the open windows. His pensive thoughts rambled over a variety of subjects. He feared the uncertain result of his lawsuit, and he was aware that there was everything to fear from the unprincipled agency employed by cunning and clever antagonists, whom he had neither the will nor the power to fight with their own weapons. And should they succeed what was to be the future? Then again he thought of the strange and unknown fate of Matangini. He had been informed of her retreat to Mathur Ghose's house, her return thence, and of her sudden disappearance. He was ignorant of the events which had driven her to seek shelter under a stranger's roof, except of what rumour gave, but Madhav knew Matangini too well to suspect that a light cause could have driven this brave-hearted girl to a step which published her own unhappiness and her failure to evince the patience of a woman and a wife. He well understood and appreciated the reasons which had deterred her from seeking

shelter in her sister's house when shelter had become necessary
to her. But he was unable to account for her leaving home,
and still less for her sudden and strange disappearance. That
Matangini had come to know of the conspiracy formed against
his property by dacoits and that she had given the timely warning
which frustrated their purpose, drove Madhav into a thousand
torturing conjectures as to her fate, but each surmise he rejected
as wild and unreasonable. Certain he was, so well did he know
her character, that whatever might have been her misfortune,
she had not been guilty of a dishonourable desertion of her
household. Assured, therefore, in his mind that she had come
by some misfortune, his heart underwent excruciating torments,
The deep and tender feeling which he had stifled in his breast
at such cost, seemed to burn with redoubled fervour. His
thoughts long dwelt on the remembrance of that parting scene;
he recalled every word that she had uttered, and tears rushed
to his eyes. Long did he muse and weep in silence. At length
he rose from his seat and, as if to forget his reflections in
the touch of the balmy air that blew outside, he went out to the
veranda. His reflections pursued him there. Leaning against
the balustrade, his head supported on the palm of his hand, his
eye fixed on the starry heavens and the range of tall devdaru
trees that stood in bold relief against the blue vault, he again lost
himself in a melancholy reverie. As he gazed and gazed, a curious
object caught his attention. A protuberance on the trunk of a
devdaru [which] stood out in relief against the sky, and on which
[he for] some time fixed his listless gaze, seemed suddenly to
vanish. It is a singular trait in the human mind that when
most intensely employed in brooding over its own gloomy
feelings, the most indifferent circumstance will sometimes
arrest its attention. The disappearance of the protruding object

on the circumference of the tree, struck Madhav as singular. He was sure that the remnant of the stem of a lopped-off branch, or a knotted protuberance on the wood, was no longer where he had seen it against the sky. Not attaching, however, any importance to the circumstance at the moment, and too busy with his own thoughts, he again resumed the subject which lay nearest his heart. A few moments after, however, his eyes again wandered to the same tree, and now he thought he could see the object once more where it was. His curiosity being now slightly awakened, he looked at it for some time with more care than before. Suddenly again the object disappeared. It distinctly exhibited motion in its disappearance. 'What can it be?' he thought. Perhaps, he surmised, it was an owl or other night-bird sleeping on its perch among twigs invisible to him in darkness and distance. Again, however, the object reappeared. Madhav could not distinguish in its form the outlines of that of either bat or bird, and it rather seemed to possess more of the shape and size of a human head than of anything else. The outlines could be clearly discerned against the sky, and he even fancied he saw part of the neck protruding from behind the tree. It appeared, however, on a height in the tree to which it was not usual for men to ascend. As the object appeared and disappeared again and again, his curiosity or apprehension or both, were excited. He thought of going to examine. Usually led on by first impulses, the thought no sooner struck him, than he decided on going himself to see who lurked behind the tree, if any did lurk. He armed himself with a small silver-handled sword that hung in his parlour, and descended the stairs. He again closely looked at the tree from his front gate, as the row of the devdarus lay very near it, but could see nothing there where he had before perceived the strange object. He looked around but without meeting with what he sought. It was therefore necessary to go to the foot of the tree. Scarcely had he reached it when a wild shriek like that of a screech owl startled him, and at the same moment his sword was wrested from him by a vigorous blow. Before he could turn to see who and where was this sudden assailant, the large and rough palm of a vigorous hand was laid upon his mouth. At the same instant a heavy body fell upon the earth from the tree, and Madhav Ghose saw before him a tall and sombre figure, vigorous and well armed.

'Bind him, this is unexpected,' said the man in a whisper to the one who had disarmed Madhav. 'Gag him first.'

The other man took out a napkin and some rope from his waist, and, gagging Madhav well with the napkin, proceeded to bind his limbs, while he who had descended from the tree, held him down. Madhav who saw the uselessness of struggling, and was powerless to call for help, quietly submitted.

'Now, take him up in your arms; you can singly carry him away,' said the latter comer in the same low tone.

The other took up Madhav in his large arms and bore off the unfortunate young man without much difficulty. The other followed, and the two left the spot without having given the smallest alarm to the household.

The Vigilance of Love

AT THE HOUR WHEN THIS STRANGE TURN OF FORTUNE OVERTOOK the hero of our tale, for such we believe the reader thinks Madhav, Mathur Ghose was resting, or, to be more accurate, endeavouring to rest in Tara's chamber. Tara was seated on the couch close by his reclining form, with a little delicate straw punkha in her hand, with which she patiently and affectionately endeavoured to lull to sleep the disturbed spirit of her husband. Her efforts, however, did not seem successful, for though Mathur was silent and his eyes closed, an occasional sigh which now and then escaped him, betrayed an anxiety of mind proceeding from some cause unknown to Tara. She at length broke silence and spoke.

'You do not sleep,' said she.

'No I cannot; this you see is not my hour to sleep.'

'Then why come to sleep at all? I fear to speak, but will you forgive me if I am bold?'

'What have you to say?'

'You are unhappy; may one who sincerely loves you learn the cause?'

Mathur gave a start. Then checking himself he answered with an assumed lightness of air which was too transparent to deceive the eyes of affection. 'Why, who told you that? What have I to grieve for?'

'Do not try to deceive me, love,' returned Tara in a tone of earnest but affectionate remonstrance. 'I know you care little for me or my love, but to a woman, her husband is—I cannot say what he is not. Deceive the world, but you cannot deceive me.'

'You are surely mad to think me wretched,' said Mathur, in a tone that most significantly contradicted his words. 'What put that fancy in you?'

'Yourself,' replied she. 'Listen: you have many things to think of; your *taluqs*,[1] your lawsuits, your rents, your *kacharis*, your houses, gardens, servants, family, and of much more: I have nothing to care for, but my husband and my daughter. Do you wonder then that for the last three days I have noted before others, that your step had lost its wonted pride? That your eyes wandered and had a strange look; that you spoke less often, and that when you smiled, your smile came not from your heart; nay, can you suppose that a mother's eye would forget to note that her child met not from its father his former warm embrace? Yes, often during these three days has Bindu held your finger, and played round your knee, and you have not spoken to her; and even my sister,' here an arch smile, which passed off as soon as it came, momentarily interrupted the earnestness of Tara's manner, 'and even my sister has pouted and stormed, and you have not listened with your wonted courtesy: and that sigh! Nay, can you longer deny that something troubles you?'

Mathur did not reply.

'Do you not think me worthy of sharing your griefs?' continued Tara, seeing that her husband did not reply. 'I know you do not love me.' Tara hesitated. Mathur still continued silent. He gazed steadfastly on the angel purity of his affectionate wife's countenance; his bosom slowly heaved, and a sigh escaped him.

'You are unhappy; conceal it not, deceive me not,' sobbed rather than uttered Tara, with an intensity of agony in the stifled tones of her voice beyond the power of language, 'deceive not, conceal not, tell me all. If my life will purchase your happiness, you can yet be happy.'

Mathur still continued mute.

He no longer jested, prevaricated, or denied, but maintained a sombre and determined [silence, and] the look of cold and hypocritical levity with [which he] was presently attempting to evade the questions [of] his wife, had given place to a serious, earnest gaze which seemed to seek and yet repel sympathy. Tears rolled down the cheek of Tara as she perceived, with a woman's sensitiveness and a woman's depth of feeling, this unusual change in the expression of her husband's face.

'Cursed be the hour of my birth!' burst from the lips of the mortified wife. 'Not even *this*! I would lay down my life to make you happy, but cursed be the hour when I was born! I cannot even know what it is that makes you unhappy.'

Mathur was touched. 'It is useless now to conceal from you that I am unhappy,' he confessed at last, 'but do not grieve that I confide not my troubles to you. Human ears will not hear them.'

As Tara heard these words, a fleeting expression of intense pain shot across her pallid but noble features, but the next moment she stood calm and apparently without emotion.

'Give me one poor request then,' said she now calmly, 'will you promise?' A wild and hollow shriek like that of a screech owl interrupted her words. Her husband started to his feet at the sound.

'Why do you start?' enquired his wife. 'It is a screech owl only, though certainly the sound was fearful to hear.'

The sound came borne once again in still more fearful notes upon the wind. Before Tara could speak Mathur bounded out of the room,

Tara was surprised. She was certain the shriek was from a screech owl, or if not, of nothing more fearful, and to her mind, there was nothing in it to apprehend except as a sound of ill omen, which, however, people daily hear and tolerate. She had also some perception that the sound they had heard, rather bore a resemblance to that of the nightbird than presented its unmistakable notes in their reality. Her curiosity was awakened, and she came out of her apartment. Finding that her husband had gone downstairs, she ascended the staircase which led to the terrace overhead in order to see what had so much startled him. Looking earnestly and long in the direction whence the sound had proceeded, she could discern nothing. Thinking therefore that the sound could have been nothing more than what it had appeared to be, and that the bird itself perhaps sat concealed in some leafy branch or invisible cornice, and also that her husband had left her in that abrupt manner only perhaps to avoid yielding to the emotion which she had seen rising palpably in his bosom, she thought the matter unworthy of further attention, and was in the act of returning, when the unusual sight of a human figure, evidently that of a man too, and not of a female inmate of the house, issuing out of the postern gate, caught her eyes. A second glance convinced Tara that it was her husband, making swiftly towards the jungles. She was staggered. A cold tremor seized her limbs, and she felt overpowered and ready to faint. A thousand vague fears and harrowing suspicions swept over her mind. She loved her unworthy husband too well to think him the agent in some dark or unhallowed purpose, but gloomy conjectures of approaching dangers and of some fearful

risk which her husband ran, rushed through her mind. She
stood riveted to the spot. Bending over the low parapet, which
surrounded the edges of the terrace, she gazed and gazed and
followed his motions with distracted eyes. Suddenly she lost all
view of him. She still gazed and turned her eyes on all sides,
but could no longer perceive his vigorous form gliding amid
the darkness. Her fears increased tenfold. Long, long did she
gaze in this attitude, silent and unmoved like a marble formed
ornament of the huge edifice. She was on the point of giving
up the [search in] despair when a last and sweeping glance met
the [object] of her solicitude as he lightly leaped into the small
iron door which opened outside from that tenantless part of
the house already known to the reader as the godown-mahal.

Tara's heart felt greatly relieved when she saw her husband
within the shelter of his own roof. Still her apprehensions were
not entirely quieted. This nocturnal and clandestine walk outside
and a visit at such an hour to a part of the house rarely visited
by any, coupled with his previous anxiety and loss of spirits and
the ominous sound of the nightbird which still rung in Tara's
ears, spoke of some approaching misfortune. Tara did not leave
her watch but continued anxiously waiting for the reappearance
of her husband. But again she watched in vain. More than half
an hour elapsed, still her husband did not repass through the
secret gate. She felt tired with standing and as she was more
sure of her husband's personal safety, she at last for the present
descended and returned to her apartment.

A sudden light had flashed upon her. Would not this furnish
a clue to her husband's secret? Her resolution was now formed.

In the course of a few moments, her husband re-entered
the room. His manner was restless and uneasy, but there
was exultation in his eyes. Tara spoke not a word to him of
what she had seen.

Captors and Captive

LET US SHIFT THE SCENE. A SOLITARY AND FEEBLE LAMP LIGHTED a gloomy and low-roofed room, whose sombre and massive walls looked more grim in the dim light. The room was as small in area as it was low in altitude, and altogether wore the appearance more of a habitation destined for the reception of criminals than of an ordinary residence of any who could find another shelter. A low small thick door of iron shut the only entrance to this gloomy apartment, and was furnished with bolts and bars of a proportionately massive character. As if still suspicious of the character of the security of this cell, the architect had taken the unusual precaution of plating the very walls with a coat of iron. The black metal frowned by the dim and flickering light as if it enclosed a living grave. There was another passage or resemblance of a passage from this room besides the iron door already mentioned. It was another door, precisely of the same character, placed in one of the corners and leading apparently to a side room; but it was even of smaller dimensions, so much so that a child had to creep through it. The gloomy apartment was without a single article of furniture. It was totally empty. One solitary individual, the sole occupant, was pacing it in the dim and fitful light of the single lamp. It was Madhav Ghose.

Our readers need not be apprised that this was the place where Madhav had been deposited by his captors. But his captors were not there. The hour was about deep midnight. The bolts were drawn outside; and Madhav Ghose for the present at least was shut up in a living grave. Still his mien was not stricken down or dejected or hopeless. Resentment more than any other feeling was foremost in his mind; and as he continued unceasingly to pace the silent chamber with a lofty step, he gathered resolution to meet the worst he had to expect from the desperate character of his captors.

At length a sound was heard of a key turning in the lock which closed the door outside. Next followed the sound of the bolt and bar and chain being cautiously unfastened, the massive doors slowly creaked on their hinges, and his two savage captors silently entered the room, shutting the door after them with the same carefulness.

Madhav cast a glance of unbounded resentment but, without taking any other notice of their entrance, continued pacing the chamber as before. The sardar and Bhiku seated themselves by the lamp, and taking out a little ganja from a bag which the latter carried in his waist, as well as a small and almost headless *kalika*, began pounding the drug on his palm by the strong pressure of his thumb, preparatory to its ignition. The sardar trimmed the lamp and, while thus employed, observed sarcastically, 'The Baboo seems particularly submissive tonight.'

Madhav stopped short in his walk, and faced the miscreant; his features worked as if he would reply, but he suddenly turned without saying anything and resumed his previous employment of pacing the chamber. The ganja was now ready for the kalika, and it being duly ignited, the robbers commenced smoking. The silent contempt of the prisoner now began to irritate his captors, who had hitherto been restrained from offering needless insult by that habitual awe and respect which compels even the most reckless among the vulgar to observe a proper distance to those entitled to deference. The sardar was no vulgar ruffian, as our readers have doubtless perceived, but the lofty mien and stern deportment of the prisoner had restrained even his petulance. But now the fumes of the ganja loosened his spirits.

'Baboo,' said he with a malicious smile on his lips, 'will you deign a pull at the kalika? It is done exactly to a millionaire's taste, I can promise you.'

Madhav again disdained replying, and the discomfited sardar went on smoking, carrying on a horribly obscene conversation with his associate.

'Will you tell me what your master intends doing with me?' at length enquired Madhav, speaking for the first time.

'We have no master,' answered the sardar gruffly, without further interruption to the smoking and the obscene dialogue.

'Your employer then?' asked Madhav again.

'We have no employer,' said the sardar in the same tone, and went on pulling at the kalika.

'He who bade you do this deed?' said Madhav.

'No one bade us,' said the sardar.

'No one? Have you seized and confined me for play?'

'Not for play,' retorted the sardar. 'We have seized and confined you for money.' The cool and collected demeanour of Madhav Ghose and the imperious tone of his language had mortified the ruffianly pride of the bandit, who piqued himself upon being the scourge and humiliator of the rich and the great, and he was resolved to be as mortifying in his answers.

'And who gives you this money?' enquired Madhav.

'Guess,' said the sardar.

'I need not.'

A deep and hollow sound interrupted the speaker and his auditors.

'What's that?' ejaculated Bhiku in amazement.

'What's that?' ejaculated the sardar in his turn.

All three remained silent for a few moments.

'Can there be another in the room? That would be a fine affair indeed,' said the sardar. 'Let me see.'

Although the whole room was visible with the distinctness that the faint light would permit from the place where they sat, the sardar nevertheless got up and scrutinized every corner, but of course with little success.

'It is strange,' he observed as he resumed his place, 'but let it go. You were speaking of my employer, sir; who do you think he is?'

The presuming tone of the question highly irritated Madhav Ghose, but suppressing his resentment he briefly answered, 'I know he is Mathur Ghose; now tell me what are your instructions.'

Bhiku gaped in surprise, and leering towards the sardar, observed, 'How is it that he knows it already?'

'Fool!' said the sardar. 'Do you gape at this, who else in Radhaganj has an iron-walled dungeon to cage his prisoners in?'

But he returned no answer to Madhav's question, true to his determination of humbling the yet lofty pride of his captive and perhaps to mould him to that state of mind which would facilitate his object. But Bhiku was getting impudent, and warmed by the fumes of the ganja, his usual taciturnity was fast giving place to an uncontrollable propensity to chatter.

'In truth,' said he, 'what are we to do with our booty: booty of flesh and blood I mean?'

'Eat him up, I suppose,' said the sardar.

Bhiku broke out into a hoarse laugh at this sally of his chief. But his rude laugh was suddenly checked by another plaintive groan which seemed to issue this time from the ceiling.

'Again!' ejaculated the startled sardar.

Bhiku sat aghast, superstitious fears now coming over him. Madhav also felt uneasy though from other causes.

'This place has been long untenanted,' observed Bhiku speaking in a whisper, 'who knows what beings may have made this room their abode.'

Though, of course, equally given to superstition, the much stronger mind of the sardar did not so easily yield to such influences. Generally, their lawless and terrible profession renders people of this class habitually conversant with those scenes which are best calculated to give rise to fears of a superhuman character, and though they as firmly believe as other ignorant people in the existence of superhuman agencies, habit renders them less liable to their impressions.

'Or somebody may be lurking somewhere,' said the sardar. 'This must be looked to; you watch our friend here.'

The sardar tore up an edge from his small dhoti and rolling it up into a wick, dipped it in the oil of the lamp, and ignited it in its flame. Thus furnished with a light, he cautiously opened the door. He then proceeded to examine every creek and corner of the veranda which lined the single row of rooms, of which the one now occupied by Madhav and his watchers was the middle one. Not finding anything in the veranda to explain the cause of his alarm he proceeded to search the open ground in front, which was enclosed by the walls already mentioned. But there also the search proved equally fruitless, and he returned vexed and doubtful. Bhiku was now really frightened and, in his anxiety to get rid of the place, gave a hard and significant pinch under the elbow of his chief to hasten negotiations. The sardar complied.

'It is getting late,' he said, addressing Madhav, 'and this

is no place for us to sleep in. If you will comply with our conditions you can regain your liberty.'

'What are they?' enquired Madhav with indifference, for he saw his advantage.

'Deliver up to us your uncle's will.'

'It is not with me here,' said he laconically, and turned round to resume his walk.

'Remain here then,' said the sardar with equal brevity; 'we go with the keys.'

'And suppose I am inclined to give up the paper, how am I to get at it from here?'

The bandit in his turn perceived his advantage, and replied, 'That is your own concern. Devise the best means in your power. If I were you I would think of sending a note by one of my captors to a friend at home, asking him to send me the paper by the bearer.'

'And if my friend asks you where is the writer of the note, what answer will you give?'

Again the same unearthly sound burst upon their ears. This time it was a low stifled shriek, such as no human being could utter. Again the sound seemed to proceed from the ceiling.

The robbers started to their feet; even Madhav himself was shaken.

'Is there an upper storey?' said he.

'No, no,' answered both the robbers at once.

'Stop; I will go up to the roof and see again,' said the sardar.

It was easy for such a practised dacoit as the sardar to scale the no great elevation of the rooms. When up, however, his search proved as fruitless as before.

Bending over the edge of the roof he gazed intently on the ground on the back of the building, but here also his search proved equally unsuccessful. He returned once more, vexed and troubled.

A sudden light broke upon Madhav.

'Are there not two other rooms, similar to this, in the row?'

'Yes,' said the sardar, 'it seems so.'

'Did you bring any other captives to these dungeons?'

'No.'

'Perhaps then others did; some unfortunate victim of this wretch's cupidity is undergoing a horrible fate in one of these cells,' said he, more as speaking to himself. 'Can you go and see if there are any there?'

'You say right,' replied the sardar, musingly. 'Probably in that case, these doors are locked; but I can speak, and the prisoner, if any there is, will doubtless reply.' The sardar again made a wick and proceeded to examine. To his great disappointment the doors of both the rooms were open and the rooms entirely empty.

Utter amazement now seized on Madhav, who clearly saw that every possible existing source had been enquired into, while the robber-chief now began seriously to give way to superstitious apprehensions.

Bhiku cowered with fear and crouched near the sardar.

'We have no heart to stay any longer,' said the sardar to Madhav. 'The ways of gods are known to themselves. Give your answer at once, or we shut you up and go.'

Madhav saw that his only chance lay in compliance. If they left him shut up, he could not guess how or when he could expect release. If he complied, it was probable that his note would cause enquiry and afford a clue to his friends by which they would trace out his place of confinement. Still he was determined to make a last effort.

'You expect money,' he said to the sardar, 'if you get the will from me; name the sum and I will double it, if you will let me go without giving up the paper.'

'We are satisfied with what has been promised to us. Who can be fool enough to think that you, once free, would give us the money you promise now. The note, or we go.'

Clothes rustled somewhere in the rooms. The dacoits looked at each other, as if ready to fly without waiting further. Madhav understood the look and enquired if they had pen and paper, to which they replied that they had come provided with them. Madhav took the pen and paper, and commenced writing a note to his chief *amla*[1] at home.

'I will dictate,' said the sardar, 'so that I may be neither doubted nor entrapped, nor your retreat found out. I could once read and write like you.'

Madhav looked up in surprise, but signified his assent and the sardar began to dictate, though from the supernatural fears which agitated him, he was far from being cool enough for the purpose. Madhav began to write.

At that moment a heavy clanking of chains, followed by a tremendous clattering sound, came thundering on the already frightened party, and then again issued the same unearthly moan, more loud and piercing. At one bound Bhiku cleared the veranda, and ran out of the house with a scream. The sardar also rose startled and leaped into the veranda. He was petrified with the vision that there met his eyes and, without turning back even to lock the door, precipitately ran out of the house, leaving Madhav entirely free.

But Madhav himself was just then too bewildered by the mysterious sounds and the sudden impetuous flight of his captors, to be able fully to comprehend his position. For a moment he remained motionless and undecided. But he was soon ashamed of himself and shaking off unmanly apprehensions jumped into the veranda. Nothing was to be seen. He looked and looked and perceived a small streak of light creeping through a crevice which opened from the veranda into the open ground. Bounding in that direction he found that the door was not locked, and throwing it open saw a female figure standing in that lonely spot. A small lantern was on the ground. Eagerly holding it up for closer examination, he was staggered at what he saw.

'Tara!' escaped from his lips.

'Madhav!' murmured Tara, speechless with astonishment. But again came [the] plaintive cry from above.

Madhav and Tara

MADHAV AND TARA HAD KNOWN EACH OTHER FROM THEIR infancy. Tara's father and Madhav's maternal grandfather were residents of the same village, and in Madhav's constant visits to the place during his boyhood, Tara had been his playmate.[1] They were distantly related to each other on this side, a circumstance which was the means of their coming so frequently in contact with each other in their early age as to be each other's playfellow. Although Tara was Madhav's senior by a few years, they had always called each other 'Tara' and 'Madhav'[2] respectively. Tara's marriage with Mathur did not to any great extent interfere to banish the feeling in the mind of each towards the other, generated by the familiar and unrestrained intercourse of infancy. For, before Mathur evinced his grasping avarice by the secret but not unperceived aid he rendered to his aunt in her lawsuit, friendly intercourse, apparently cordial on both sides, had subsisted between the cousins, and necessarily Madhav's visits to Mathur's household were frequent. By so many years the junior of Mathur, zenana etiquette did not stand in the way of his holding frequent conversations with Tara on these occasions, and Madhav always availed himself of every such opportunity. Such an intercourse was equally gratifying to both, for each had a high esteem for the other. But their mutual fondness, and such the feeling might suitably be termed, was far removed from all impurity of the heart. Their attachment to each other springing in childhood, and nurtured by a daily growing appreciation of the moral beauty of each other's heart, had ripened into an affection that was akin to the love of brother and sister.

Nevertheless, when Tara and Madhav found themselves face to face in the godown-mahal, their situation was sufficiently embarrassing. Surprise at this strange and, to both, inexplicable meeting, was the first feeling that predominated in their minds. When its effects had subsided, they began to feel the embarrassing character of their situation, and for some time neither spoke. Tara first broke the silence. 'You here, Madhav!'

Madhav could not well retort the interrogatory on Tara, but remained silent, hardly knowing how to answer. Tara felt all the novelty and embarrassment of the situation; but in such cases women, perhaps, are better able to get over the difficulty than men. Tara, confident in the integrity of her own character and feeling secure from misapprehension on the part of the other, in the esteem she knew Madhav entertained for her, as well as sensible of the necessity of coming to an explanation, proceeded to bring matters to an issue.

'First, tell me, Thakurpo,[3] who could be the two Jama-dut-like men who just now ran away from here? I wonder what business you could have had with people of that description, and here in our house too? One of them gazed at me fixedly when I stood there in the veranda, and perhaps taking me for a ghost fled precipitately.'

'Was it you then who opened this door and clanked the chains?'

'Yes, I opened the door, and was making towards the room from which you came out, but the appearance of these Jama-duts frightened me, and I was returning.'

'And whence came the sounds?'

'What sounds?'

'Have you heard nothing strange?'

'Yes, a freezing shriek of woe; but I thought it was coming from your room.'

'No.'

'No? You frighten me. I shall return.'

'Without hearing; hearing why I am here?'

'I must hear it, and I must also tell you why I came here. Be quick then.'

'Gladly,' replied Madhav, 'but I must take some precautions from interruption which you will by and by understand.'

Madhav went out, and drew the massive bar of the door which led from the godown-mahal at once out of the house. He then re-entered the apartment which had so lately been his prison, and beckoning to Tara to follow, sat down to narrate the history of his capture. He neither concealed nor extenuated any circumstance, speaking as he did in the bitterness of resentment, as well as from a consciousness that however affectionately Tara might love her husband, she was too pure-minded herself to sympathize with his crooked policy. Tara felt sorely grieved as well as disappointed.

'You are not then what I seek,' she said. 'You have arrived only this evening, while I believe my suspicions were roused two days ago.'

Tara related in her turn the purpose of her visit. That need not be detailed to the reader. He has already seen with what solicitude this affectionate wife had watched the change in her husband; how she had racked her mind with fruitless conjectures for its cause; how at last she had importuned her husband for a disclosure, and how disappointed she had been in her wishes; how at last the strange and secret walk her husband had taken that night, and his clandestine and mysterious entry into the godowns, had raised suspicion in her mind that the mysterious cause of her solicitude lay concealed in that apartment; how she determined to wrest the secret at all hazards and to visit the godowns that night, to know what misfortune lay hid beneath its roof; and lastly, how she had secured the keys from her husband while he slept, from beneath his pillow.

'How many fears, what tremor, what anxiety,' continued Tara, 'assailed me as, possessed of the stolen keys I threaded my dark way beneath these sombre walls, you can better conceive than I describe. But I felt myself acting under a supernatural impulse and came on. I could have died if my death would have removed his unhappiness. Judge then what impression your presence here made on me. I at once connected your presence here, with the cause of his unhappiness. But you say you are here only from this evening. You cannot then be what I seek.'

'You will not perhaps be disappointed,' said Madhav in reply, shuddering as he spoke. 'Those sounds—did you not hear them? There is a mystery yet to solve.'

Tara turned pale.

'Do not be frightened,' said Madhav. 'I believe there is nothing to fear, I will relate what I have just heard and seen. I will do so, however, only if you give me a promise not to indulge in a woman's fears. Do you promise?'

It was with difficulty that she gasped out the words, 'Speak on.' Madhav then gave her an account of the strange sounds that had interrupted his interview with the dacoits, relieving her by the tone of his narrative as much of supernatural fears, as the nature of the subject admitted.

Tara's feelings were most painful. Fear, natural in women[4] whom philosophy never taught to disbelieve in supernatural beings, predominated. Mingled with it, was curiosity, such as danger excites, and an intense regret that her search should be attended with so much terror. She now almost repented having undertaken it, and asked Madhav to see her safe to the interior of the house.

'Will you give up your search so easily? I assure you there is no danger,' said Madhav with some vehemence, for his curiosity and interest had been intensely awakened, and he had forgotten his own precarious, and with Tara in his company, delicate situation, for its gratification.

Tara remained silent for some moments. Mustering resolution at last, she replied, 'Where can we search? Have not the robbers searched everywhere?'

'Yes, but I see now that one thing escaped them. There is a door,' he said, pointing to the little iron door we have described before, 'which remained to be opened.'

'It evidently leads to the other room: did not they examine that other room also?'

At this moment, again came the hollow agony-bespeaking sound, clearer, more distinct than ever. The listeners started; its touching and startling tones thrilled them in every nerve.

A short pang shot across Madhav's brain. A dark and agonizing thought seized him. Wrenching almost with violence the bunch of keys from Tara's hand, he madly sprung towards the little door, knelt down, and pushed a key into the keyhole. It did not turn. With the same vehemence of movement he tried a second and a third key, but with the same ill-success. Maddened with vexation, and the torture of suspense, he would have torn open the ponderous metal, had he the strength. Happily for his self-command, the fourth key he tried turned in the lock, and away flew the heavy door as though it were a feather.

'Tara! Tara! Hesitate not, but follow,' he said, with compressed energy, and crept in, bruising his sides.

Led by the contagion of impulse, Tara followed with the light. Joy and surprise held Madhav mute when they discerned a staircase of brick, narrow and deep, and filled with spiders' webs. Without stopping to speak Madhav bounded up, and Tara lost in amazement, mechanically continued to follow. The staircase led to a small door of apparently an upper-storeyed room. A glance at the very small height of this room sufficed to convince Madhav of the art with which it had been so made as to be concealed from every other part of the building. He saw that the height of the two rooms, upper and lower together, made up the height of the side rooms and the veranda, and being destitute of windows the existence of the upper storey could not possibly be discerned from any other part of the building, nor any way suspected except by a comparison of the height of the central room with that of the adjacent ones.

Madhav, anxious and trembling, sought the lock of this second door and, after two or three fruitless attempts in which the violent movement of the keys brought blood from his fingers, he succeeded, and threw open the plated door ringing and echoing. Tara entered with him, holding the light in her hand. The feeble glimmer it threw around, revealed to them an unexpected sight. Upon a small bedstead of varnished mahogany, splendidly ornamented with gauze and crepe,[5] lay a form apparently that of a female. Tara and Madhav ran to the bedstead with the light; and its dim and ghastly glare, as Tara held it over the bedstead, revealed to them the features—pale emaciated agonized, but still heavenly—the features of MATANGINI.

Some Women Are the Equals
of Some Men

TARA AND MADHAV BORE AWAY THE SEEMINGLY LIFELESS MATANGINI to an apartment which was secure from interruption. The exertions of Tara, materially aided by the wholesome fresh air to which Matangini had been for so many days a stranger, soon recalled the blood to her face, and long before the first streaks of day had brightened the eastern sky, Matangini was again a living being. Refreshments were provided for her, but she ate little. The little she did eat considerably revived her, and as Tara sat on the window eyeing the grey light in the east, Matangini softly and slowly unfolded to her the course of the painful events which had nearly consigned her to a living grave.

Briefly told, that dark story is this: When Mathur Ghose sent her home in Suki's mother's company, Matangini had no suspicion of the snare which had been laid for her by that wily monster. Suki's mother, who had been well instructed in her part, asked her on the way if she had no apprehension in returning to her husband.

'To tell you the truth, Sukir-ma,' replied Matangini, 'I would not go, if earth held a place where I could remain.'

'Would you?' asked the wretch. 'I think I can serve you. I would conceal you in a place where nobody could find you out.'

'No,' said Matangini thoughtfully, 'I must not conceal myself. Evil tongues will be busy.'

'Then why not come to your sister's house?'

Matangini heaved a deep sigh. 'No! that is not to be thought of.'

The artful woman appeared to sympathize sincerely with her helpless situation, and at length suggested embarking for her father's house.

'How am I to find the means?' said Matangini sorrowfully.

'Oh! As for that, I dare say my elder mistress will find you a boat if she knew you wished it; and I can accompany and leave you there.'

Matangini wept, anticipating this act of kindness on Tara's part.

'Shall I go and tell her?'

'Yes,' said Matangini, joyfully.

'You then wait where I leave you till I come back. There no one will observe you. Come.'

Matangini went where the woman-fiend led. She led her to the little room above-stairs in the godown-mahal. The sombre and deserted appearance of the rooms shot a chill through her heart as she passed the approaches. She was surprised to find the deserted dark little room splendidly furnished. She turned to Suki's mother to explain the mystery. Lo! Suki's mother had vanished, bolting the door after her!

Matangini's intelligent mind now comprehended everything. Her resolution was formed at once with her usual promptitude.

In the evening, Mathur Ghose came and laid himself at her feet. The indignantly contemptuous repulse he met with, wounded and mortified him. He determined to gratify at once both revenge and lust.

'You shall be mine yet, life,' said Mathur, as with a demoniacal look he was departing for that evening.

'Never!' said Matangini, concentrating the energy of twenty

men in her look. 'Never *yours*. Look here;' and she placed herself immediately in front of him. 'Look; I am a full-grown woman, and at least *your* equal in brute force. Will you call in allies?' Mathur Ghose stood bewildered at this wonderful challenge.

'Hunger shall be my ally. I lift not a finger against a woman,' said Mathur, recovering himself.

'Hunger shall be my ally,' said Matangini, in return.

Mathur had resolved to starve her to compel her compliance. Matangini had resolved to starve herself to be rid from his power.

Both kept their word. Mathur visited her daily, to watch the effect. Matangini was literally starving when Madhav rescued her.

Madhav departed before it was quite daylight. Matangini was too feeble to be immediately removed, and it was arranged between Madhav and Tara that Tara should keep her concealed till the ensuing night, when Karuna would come to fetch her.

After seeing Madhav safe out of the house, Tara returned to Matangini, and observing playfully that it was now her turn to make her a captive, locked the door of the chamber to deceive appearances. She then returned to her husband's apartment, replaced the bunch of keys whence she had purloined them, and went to bed as if not a mouse had stirred during the night. Did she sleep? No! She had now learnt her husband's secret, and a terrible acquisition of knowledge it had proved to her noble heart. Perhaps of all the visitors in the scenes of that eventful night, none had suffered so deeply as the affectionate and confiding wife, appalled by the unexpected disclosures of the dark deeds of her husband.

Matangini spent the day in her safe but solitary chamber. Late in the evening Karuna came, as had been arranged, and at length, after so much suffering and wretchedness, Matangini had the pleasure of clasping Hemangini to her bosom.

'And you will never leave me again, sister, will you?' said Hem, after her joy at the meeting had subsided a little.

Matangini sighed. There were tears in her eyes.

'Why don't you answer?' asked Hemangini, a little impatiently.

'Alas! I fear we must part!'

'And for whom will you leave me?' said Hem, disappointed.

'I go to MY FATHER,' said Matangini.

The Last Chapter in Life's
Book — and In This

THE EVENING THAT FOLLOWED WAS A TEMPESTUOUS AND GLOOMY one. The wind howled, the rain fell in torrents, and the thunder rattled loud and long. As Mathur Ghose sat alone, a sound like that of blowing at a conch-shell fell on his ears, during intermissions in the violence of the storm. Twice he could distinctly hear it. His first thought was not to obey the well-known signal of those whose unworthy association had just brought on him infamy and disgrace. But every time that the sound was heard it became louder and louder, and more and more urgent. At length he left his seat, and braving the storm, repaired to the spot which had been the scene of so many of his dark interviews. A form lurked beneath a tree, and he had no difficulty in recognizing it to be that of the robber-chief.

'What brings you now here?' said he, pettishly. 'I have had enough of you. Rid me of your presence. My good name is lost, and your treachery the cause.'

'I do not deserve this reproach,' replied the robber, calmly; 'we did our best. He who takes us for his associates must abide by the consequences.'

The scoundrel was preaching philosophy to the great man! And, dear reader, was he very wrong?[1]

'But our connection has ceased,' rejoined Mathur, angrily; 'you know it well enough. Why do you seek me at this stormy hour?'

'Because,' said the sardar, mournfully, 'because this is the only hour when I can dare come out now. The police are after us, as you know.'

'Then, why not rid Radhaganj of your presence at once?'

'You were not wont to speak thus to us, Baboo,' said the sardar, with a slight touch of his old manner, 'when these days had not come over us. Think as you may, I am come to convince you that we have a better memory than you suppose of those whom we serve, or those who serve us.'

'What do you mean?' asked Mathur.

'You do not see with me tonight, one who used to follow me as my shadow,' answered the sardar with a shade of melancholy.

'Yes—where is that man? Bhiku you call him, I believe?'

'In the hands of the police.'

Mathur was startled. 'Nothing worse?' asked he, tremblingly.

'Alas! Yes!' replied the sardar in a desponding[2] tone. 'He has confessed.'

'Confessed *what*?' asked Mathur with furious anxiety.

'Much,' said the sardar with the same despondency, 'much that may send *both you and me* across the black waters. *Me* they shall not catch. This hour is my last at Radhaganj. But you have done well by us, and it shall never be said we did ill by you. So I came to give you a warning.'

So saying the bandit vanished into the thicket without waiting for a reply.

Mathur Ghose turned back and regained the house. For a couple of hours he sat musing deeply. His was a strong mind, and speedily regained courage. The police was venal and corrupt;[3] his wealth was vast; he would buy up the police. There was one hitch in the scheme. A shrewd and restlessly active Irishman[4] sat in the district station as magistrate, and it was his besetting sin to be meddling with everything. He was constantly shaking out ugly affairs of the police. But Mathur Ghose promised himself to see that Bhiku should recant before the meddlesome Irishman.

His meditations were interrupted by someone bounding into the room, dripping with rain, and bespattered with mud. It was one of his trustworthy agents employed in the zila courts.

'Fly, master, fly!' said the man. 'You have not a moment to lose.'

'How so?' asked Mathur, bewildered at this new warning.

'One Bhiku has this day at eleven o'clock confessed to the magistrate to dacoities and other crimes committed, as he falsely said, at your instigation.'

'Confessed to the magistrate?' repeated Mathur, almost mechanically, turning pale as death.

'Yes,' said the law-agent, 'and I started immediately after the confession was worded. I saw the saheb making preparations for starting, and I am afraid he will be at Radhaganj during the course of the night.'

'At Radhaganj during the course of the night?' again iterated Mathur, mechanically.

'Fly, sir! Immediately!' repeated the man.

'Yes; go,' said Mathur, mechanically again.

The man went away.

Next morning the busy Irishman came to Mathur Ghose's house, to arrest him personally, a whole posse of policemen following at his heels in a hundred varieties of dress, and an eager rabble pressing close upon them to have a peep at the sort of animal they call a magistrate, and the pranks he liked to play. Arrived at the house, it was entered, and thoroughly ransacked for the owner, but he was not to be found. At length found he was. There in the godown-mahal, in the very room which had formed the prison of Madhav and so many others of his victims, the master of the house was found—DEAD. He had hanged himself.

Conclusion[1]

AND NOW, GOOD READER, I HAVE BROUGHT MY STORY TO A close. Lest, however, you fall to censuring me for leaving your curiosity unsatisfied, I will tell you what happened to the other persons who have figured in this tale.

The sardar successfully escaped—not so Rajmohan. He had been implicated deeply in Bhiku's confession,—was apprehended, and under the hope of a pardon confessed likewise. They were, however, wise by half and made only partial confessions. The pardon was revoked, and both he and Bhiku transported.

Matangini could not live under Madhav's roof. This, of course, they both understood. So intimation was sent to her father and he came and took her home. Madhav increased the pension he allowed the old man, on her account. History does not say how her life terminated, but it is known that she died an early death.

Tara mourned in solitude the terrible end of a husband who had proved himself so little worthy of her love. She lived a long widowhood in repose, and, when she died, died mourned by many.

As to Madhav, Champak and the rest, some are dead, and the others will die. Throwing this flood of light on their past and future history, I bid you, good reader, Farewell.

Afterword

IT IS WELL KNOWN THAT AFTER *RAJMOHAN'S WIFE* (1864) Bankimchandra Chattopadhyay abandoned his creative project in English altogether and went on to write fourteen influential novels and a great deal of discursive prose in Bangla, which made him not only the most prominent literary figure of nineteenth-century Bengal, but a major protagonist in India's intellectual history, one who continues to be vigorously read, interpreted and debated upon even a century after his death. Quite apart from the vast quantities of commentaries on Bankimchandra's work that exist in Bangla, in the last decade or so several historians and literary scholars have begun to write on him in English.[1] They demonstrate how Bankimchandra's novels serve as productive sites for studying the complex, and often contradictory, configurations of the colonial mind, as also for understanding the process in which the emergent notion of national identity was constructed through fictional rewritings of history. His Bangla novels—those set in the past as well as in his own time—are constantly being reinterpreted and deconstructed from new perspectives—for example, feminist theory or colonial discourse—to unravel fresh layers of meaning, and even the silences and ellipses in the text are made to reveal cultural anxieties.

But his only novel in English has left behind no such wake. We have no evidence of what his contemporary readers thought of the novel, or whether anyone read it at all in the century that followed. Those interested in the history of Indian writing in English know about the existence of the novel, but even for them it has been little more than a dead entry carried over from one bibliography to another, without anyone trying to exhume the corpse, or attempting to perform a post-mortem. Even those critics who made dismissive references to the novel, designating it as 'a false start', seldom took the trouble to explain what exactly was wrong with it.[2]

When Bankimchandra died in 1894, his younger contemporary Aurobindo Ghose (later Sri Aurobindo) wrote a series of seven commemorative pieces on him in a Bombay-based journal, *Induprakash*, in which he casually mentioned this novel but only as evidence to prove his favourite thesis: 'To be original in an acquired language is hardly feasible.' According to Ghose (who himself, incidentally, only wrote in English), for an Indian, the enterprise of writing in English has 'something unnatural and spurious about it—like speaking with a stone in the mouth or walking with stilts'.[3] Bankimchandra's English novel seems to have inspired little critical observation beyond such sweeping assertions. Out of the seventy-five essays included in the massive 700-page centenary volume *Bankimchandra: Essays in Perspective* published by the Sahitya Akademi in 1994, not one focuses on *Rajmohan's Wife*, and the few incidental references to it found in the pages of this book merely reiterate the opinions expressed in the past.[4]

II

Rajmohan's Wife was Bankim's initial and tentative attempt to write fiction based on a Victorian narrative model to which colonial education had exposed a new generation of urban Indians. Independently, similar attempts were being made in several Indian languages in the second half of the nineteenth century.[5] Although literary historians have cited different and contesting dates for the first Indian novel, it may be safe to say that when *Rajmohan's Wife* was written, the novel was still a new and malleable genre in India. Only two years after his stillborn English text Bankim wrote his first work of fiction in Bangla, *Durgeshnandini* (1866), whose success was resounding, and the reverberations continued for several decades: the novel was reprinted, dramatized and emulated in Bangla repeatedly and was subsequently translated or adapted in several other Indian languages. Set in the late sixteenth century, *Durgeshnandini* depicts the conflict between a Mughal emperor of Delhi and his subedar in Bengal, evoking the extravagance, colour and the imaginative intensity of a romance. The romance mode, blended with history, continued to be a dominant strand in the narrative fiction of several Indian languages— in Bangla, Hindi and Marathi, for example— till the end of the nineteenth century.

Rajmohan's Wife, which pre-dates Bankim's success in the romance mode, had attempted a realistic representation of contemporary Bengali life, modified no doubt by the pulls of other narrative traditions: Sanskrit kavya (for example, in the metaphor-laden description of female beauty— 'charm as that of the land-lotus half scorched and half radiant by the noon-day'), or the Gothic novel (in the evocation of terror: dark dungeons lit by 'a solitary and feeble lamp' while 'massive doors creaked on their hinges'). *Rajmohan's Wife* prefigures some of the concerns that surface later in Bankim's subsequent Bangla novels when he returns to realism and to contemporary life—the stealing of a will (*Krishnakanter Will*, 1876), extra-marital passion (*Visha-briksha*, 1873), female initiative (*Indira*, 1873), childhood attachment growing into adolescent love

(*Chandrashekhar*, 1875), and several other less-worked-out motifs. Yet this novel has never been read and remembered as these others have been. The different receptions accorded to Bankim's English novel and his novels in Bangla raise several interlinked questions. Was *Rajmohan's Wife* a false start because the author chose to write in English, or was it because it deployed a narrative mode which, for whatever reason, turned out to be unsuitable for his purpose at that moment? Does choice of language—hence inescapably, of audience—inadvertently condition the semantic connotations of a text or implicitly determine its ideological base? As the novel was being serialized, was the writer himself affected by the awareness of the lack of a sizeable reading community, a suspicion that gets confirmed by the author's declining involvement in the events of the novel in the later chapters and an undue sense of haste at the end? In literary discourse causes and effects can never be conclusively established but questions like these will be further explored in the brief analysis of the novel that is attempted here.

III

The elaborate unfolding of the plot and the intricate relationships among the dramatis personae create the impression that *Rajmohan's Wife* was intended to be a longer novel than it actually turned out to be. The dyadic introduction of the characters in the first two chapters (two women in one and two men in the other, with sharply contrasting attributes and sartorial details in each case), and the depiction of Matangini's misery in the third, is followed by a long and complicated genealogical flashback whose purpose might have been to provide hereditary or environmental justification for the behaviour patterns of the characters. Mathur and Madhav are collaterals descended from a scheming ancestor who appropriated money through dubious means to rise in society. Though the author does not state this explicitly, Mathur's crudity may be attributed to his half-baked village education (we are told his father condemned an English school 'as a thing not only useless, but positively mischievous'), while Madhav's refinement may be the result of the English education he received in Calcutta. Madhav's father was actually attracted to the city by the luxury and profligacy Calcutta promised to young men with money, but the unexpected by-product of this move was the exposure of his son to the new liberal humanist ethos of English education. The dialogic myth of Calcutta that was to evolve through the nineteenth century (the city as a site for culture and refinement as well as for debauchery and moral degradation) is already quite visible here, as for example in the conversation between Mathur and Madhav in 'The Two Cousins' and later in the women's talk about rural and urban hairstyles in 'Between Rival Charmers'.

In many of Bankimchandra's Bangla novels the English-knowing urban dilettante is the butt of the author's ridicule (for example, Debendra in *Krishnakanter Will*), but in *Rajmohan's Wife* Madhav's knowledge of English and his Calcutta background are set up as signs of moral superiority over Mathur who stares at the women as they return from the river carrying water, indulges in bawdy gossip and uses illegal means to satisfy his craving for money. At a crucial moment in the narrative we find Madhav Ghose reclining on a 'mahogany couch covered with satin. A single but well-fed light illumined the chamber. Some two or three English books were scattered over the couch and one of them Madhav held in his hand . . .' The

English books are obviously signifiers of a more civilized way of life—as is the Western furniture—to which Mathur Ghose, despite his money, power and 'mofussil magnificence' can never aspire. In Mathur's bedchamber the varnish of the almirahs and chests has been 'considerably . . . soiled by time and rough usage' and the walls are decorated with two large paintings 'from one of which glowered the grim black figure of Kali and the other . . . displayed the crab-like form of Durga'. The unusually negative charge in the description of the goddesses is surprising because in Bankim's Bangla writing we never find these icons treated in such a dismissive manner. These instances make one return to the question posited earlier— how much does the choice of the writer's language (hence of audience) determine his tone and attitude?

While in most of Bankimchandra's Bangla novels the Englishman is either the abductor or the adversary (for example, Lawrence Forester in *Chandrashekhar*, Captain Thomas in *Anandamath*, the Lieutenant Saheb in *Debi Chaudhurani*), in *Rajmohan's Wife* the white man is ascribed a positive and stabilizing function. When the seemingly invincible local alliance of patriarchy, criminality and money more or less destroys Matangini by the end of the novel, the only redressal, almost as divine retribution, comes from the fair-minded white administrator—'a shrewd and restlessly active Irishman'. This unquestioning faith in colonial justice surfaces only very intermittently in nineteenth-century Bangla fiction—as, for example, in Rabindranath Tagore's short story 'Didi'— deftly analysed by Gayatri Chakraborty Spivak,[6] but more often than not British rule is perceived as oppressive and exploitative. Certainly nowhere in Bankimchandra's Bangla corpus do we find the justice and efficiency of imperial rule so unequivocally, if briefly, proclaimed as in his solitary English novel, *Rajmohan's Wife*.

The criminals are duly punished at the end of the novel, but even the British legal system is powerless to redeem Matangini. When in the last chapter just deserts are meted out to all the characters according to the conventions of British Victorian novels, Matangini poses a problem for the author. She cannot be returned to the conjugal space from which she has dislodged herself through an emotionally sanctioned but socially unforgivable act. Sending her back to her parents' home is a temporary solution, after which an early death becomes expedient for the tidiness of the closure as well as the resolution of the author's own moral dilemma. By making her confess her love for a person not her husband, the author has pushed Matangini into an uncharted and ambiguous territory from which neither romantic sympathy nor colonial justice can deliver her to a positive future. The object of her love— Madhav—has been refined by his English education into such a paragon of scrupulous virtue that, when Matangini confronts him with her passion, all he can do is to weep and implore her to forget him. Matangini is impetuous and brave, but the author weighs down her confession with a rhetoric of guilt ('sinful', 'impure felicity', 'you cannot hate me more than I hate myself', etc.) so that she already stands condemned. Whatever may have been the author's moral design, despite his correctness of conduct, the passive and indecisive Madhav gets quite overshadowed in this text by the fiery heroine.

Matangini is the first in a series of strong and transgressive women in Bankimchandra's novels (Ayesha in *Durgeshnandini*, Rohini in *Krishnakanter Will*, Shaibalini in *Chandrashekhar* are some of the others), who have to be relentlessly punished even though the author and the reader may understand and admire their rebellion. Women's agency is foregrounded, but with a simultaneous reminder of the disruptive social potential of its assertive aspect. Characterization is not Bankim's forte in this apprentice novel. Matangini only occasionally gets illuminated as a character. The other characters remain sketchy by and large, but what really disturbs the reader is the abruptness of the end: 'As to Madhav, Champak and the rest, some are dead and the others will die. Throwing this flood of light on their past and future history, I bid you, good reader, Farewell.'

This breezy assertion of universal mortality in retrospect makes all storytelling redundant. But such an ending could be the author's way of getting out of a serialization project that was no longer engaging his interest.

IV

The suffering of women is central to *Rajmohan's Wife* and it tended to be one of the major concerns in Indian fiction for several decades to come. Not only do half of Bankimchandra's novels have women as protagonists, but many of his contemporary novelists in Bengal and other parts of India focused on women and their predicament. From the first Marathi novel *Yamuna Paryatan* (1857), to its late nineteenth-century successor *Pan Lakshyant Kon Gheto* (1890), from the early Hindi novel *Devrani Jethani ki Kahani* (1870) to Premchand's *Nirmala* (1926), the examples can be multiplied from almost any Indian language.[7]

It is not entirely a coincidence that several major European novels of the nineteenth century also have women as their protagonists (for example, *Emma, Vanity Fair, Jane Eyre, Madame Bovary, Anna Karenina, Middlemarch, Portrait of a Lady, Tess*).

Classic realism, which was the dominant fictional mode of
the time, attempted to convey in concrete and specific details
the complex relationship between individuals and the society
by whose code they were expected to live. The resultant tension
could be studied in sharper contours when the protagonist's life
was restricted within a narrow space with very few options
regarding mobility, economic self-sufficiency or vocation—in
other words, when the protagonist was a woman. In most
cultures, social conformity has always been more obligatory for
a woman than for a man, her identity generally constructed—
by herself as much as by others—in terms of her relationship
with men as daughter, wife, mother or widow. Although in the
present novel Rajmohan interests us very little as a person,
Matangini's identity, as announced in the title, is irrevocably
connected to her marital status.

Apart from this beautiful and spirited woman wasted on
a brutal and surly husband, there are other female characters
in the novel—Kanak, married to an absent and polygamous
husband who, according to the custom of Kulin Brahmans, is
not obliged to provide her with a home, and Tara, the wife of
a powerful landlord, superseded in her husband's affection by a
younger and prettier wife—providing three variations on
the theme of wifely misery. Compared to some of the
magnificent later heroines of Bankimchandra's Bangla novels—
Kapalkundala, Prafulla or Shanti—these women seem somewhat
perfunctorily sketched, but they certainly engage our attention
more than the men in this novel who are either meekly virtuous
or melodramatically villainous. The scenes around the
women, specially the vivid descriptions of group activities in
the interiors of the houses, contribute to the reading pleasure
of the novel, evoking an ethos that is vibrant with life. Two

chapters stand out. The mock-serious account of the bustle and commotion in the kitchen courtyard in 'A Letter—a Visit to the Zenana' where cooks, servant women, children and girls with tinkling ankle-bells vie with each other to keep the decibel level permanently high; and a more relaxed scene in 'Between Rival Charmers', when the slanting rays of the late afternoon sun fall at regular intervals through the balcony rails in an upstairs veranda where women sit around dressing each others' hair or painting their feet with 'lac dye', discussing the different ways of braiding hair in Radhaganj and Calcutta, reiterating a recurring concern of the novelist—the relative merits of rural East Bengal and the urbanized West Bengal dominated by Calcutta. But both these engaging scenes are suddenly shattered by the unexpected arrivals of the masters of the houses, abruptly silencing the women into awe and making them scurry and hide from the authoritarian male gaze. In positions of absolute power, the masters of the house, depending on their mood, can order instant obedience, punish defiance or confer favour. Compared to this predictable man—woman relationship, the equations among the women across the classes have a more nuanced texture in the novel—of mutual bonding, subtle rivalry, friendship, sympathy or betrayal. Suki's mother and Karuna, domestic servants both, become, within the limited frame of this brief novel, as concretely realized as the landlord's wives.

The mood of the novel changes very fast and frequently. Domestic disharmony, legal intrigue, criminal conspiracy, passionate but forbidden love and dark incarceration in dungeons alternate in rapid succession. One of the most memorable of its many shifting scenes is Matangini's solitary journey in the dark night through forest, water, storm and lightning, redolent with literary echoes of Radha's *abhisara* in Vaishnava poetry, when she braved the elements to meet Krishna secretly. Where Matangini lets her long hair loose in the water of the pond around her fair face to avoid detection in the moonlight, in this rootedness in a recognizable literary culture we catch a glimpse of what Bankim would be able to achieve when he would no longer be inhibited by the anxiety of tailoring his sensibility to suit the cloth of English idioms and metaphors.

V

Bankimchandra's English novel was quite evidently hampered by the absence of the range of registers available to him in his Bangla writing—from the sonorous Sanskritic or heavily Persianized diction to the earthy raciness of Prakrit and the vitality of local dialects. In English he had by and large one linguistic code at his disposal—the formal literary style to which his class of men had been exposed through two generations of English education. Bankimchandra Chattopadhyay was one of seven students in the first graduating batch when the University of Calcutta was set up. Before he went up to Hoogly College he had already studied English for six years under the tutelage of two Englishmen—Stydd and Sinclair, in Midnapore School. While studying English in college he started publishing poetry in Bangla journals like *Sambad Prabhakar* and *Sambad Sudhiranjan*, but he chose English for his first sustained piece of prose—which was written six years after he came out of college. Bangla did not have a model of novel writing at that time—he was obviously emulating examples from English literature—but the tradition of poetry was long and alive in Bengal. As it turned out in the long run, however, neither poetry in Bangla nor fiction in English was going to be his true metier.

After joining government service as a Deputy Magistrate Bankim appears to have stopped writing in Bangla for a few years. His first attempt at writing after he began his official career seems to have been made at the request of Kishori Chand Mitra, who might have been Bankim's colleague in the Bengal Civil Service, had he not been dismissed around the time that Bankim had his first posting in Khulna. It seems curious that the dismissed civil servant, an active member of various social reform organizations and the brother of Pearey Chand Mitra who is remembered as the author of the first novel in Bangla, should decide to start a journal in English, and not in Bangla. It is in this short-lived and small-circulation journal *Indian Field* that *Rajmohan's Wife* was serialized in 1864.

'English education' by this time had begun to assume a unique role in the lives of the Calcutta elite, as also in the lives of similar men in the other metropolitan areas of India. The University of Bombay was started in 1858 along with the universities of Calcutta and Madras, and in 1882 Krishna Vishnu Chiplunkar wrote, 'Crushed by English poetry . . . our freedom was destroyed',[8] using poetry in a moment of creative clarity as a synecdoche for the entire range of Western influences. Yet at the same time English poetry was also perceived as a liberating agent rather than an enslaving force. Rabindranath Tagore wrote about his responses to Shakespeare and Shelley: '. . . our hearts naturally craved the life-bringing shock of the passionate emotions expressed in English literature. Ours was not the aesthetic enjoyment of literary art, but the jubilant welcome of a turbulent wave from a situation of stagnation . . .'[9]

This ambivalence towards English literature and what it stood for continued through the nineteenth century, and possibly also later.

Meanwhile, the word 'education' had come to be synonymous with English education, of which the study of English literature comprised a major part. In the words of Nirad C. Chaudhuri:

From the second quarter of the nineteenth century, the word education which had passed into Bengali speech, sometimes in the contracted form of 'ejoo', was applied only to those who knew English well, and never to anyone else, however learned he may be in Sanskrit or Bengali. A profound scholar who might have been a great authority on Vedanta philosophy, would have been called a Pundit, but never an educated man.[10]

This had behavioural implications among the urban Bengali male (with a few notable exceptions, women in the nineteenth century were not part of the charmed circle of the 'educated') even outside literary and intellectual domains. It is sometimes assumed that while English was becoming the language of formal and public discourse, Bangla remained the language of intimacy and personal relationships. But there is enough evidence from the nineteenth century to indicate that frequently English was the language of informal correspondence as well, if not of conversation, when both parties happened to know English. Michael Madhusudan Dutt, long after his dramatic abandonment of English as his language of creative expression, continued to write letters to his friends in English about his personal concerns.[11] In another part of India we have the example of Govardhandas Tripathi who kept a detailed personal diary in English to record the many unresolved conflicts of his life, while he earned fame and eminence by writing the massive four-volume novel *Saraswatichandra* (1887–1900) in Gujarati.

Letters between fathers and sons tended to be in English when both were 'educated', and Nirad C. Chaudhuri with his unerring eye for cultural incongruities observes how Bangla almanacs, normally consulted for astrological information necessary for regulating daily life, came by the end of the century also to include model letters in English for the use of fathers and sons. As an example of how language can transform modes of thought and behaviour, he cites one such letter where, in response to a request for more money from the son studying in Calcutta, the father writes: 'Your mother, like myself, feels grieved' at such extravagance. Chaudhuri comments:

No Hindu father would refer to the mother in discussing money matters with his son and if he did, it would be 'I and your mother' rather than 'your mother and I' which the language necessitates. We could not write in English without changing mentally. We could not merely pay the tithe of mint and anise and cumin to the language and omit the weightier matter of revising our attitudes towards our wives and husbands.[12]

It may not be easy to determine how much of this revision was merely a matter of surface adjustment to temporarily accommodate the demands of English phrasaeology, and how much actually percolated to the level of perception or consciousness. This question occasionally surfaces while we read *Rajmohan's Wife*. When an unsophisticated village woman of East Bengal is made to exclaim 'Go to Jericho!' as a phrase of friendly remonstrance, or when the author chooses certain lexical items external to the ethos of the story (for example, 'olive' to describe a woman's complexion, or 'Billingsgate' to

describe low or vituperative language) the reader is troubled
by the possibility that a second-hand and bookish mind-frame
is regulating expression. A more serious question about the
compatibility between culture and language arises when
Matangini is made to articulate her illicit love for her brother-
in-law in the passionate language of Romantic poetry.

After *Rajmohan's Wife*, Bankim never attempted to write
imaginative literature in English, though he continued to
write essays and discursive pieces in English and actively
participated in various debates about religion and culture in
the columns of local English newspapers. He was the second
major example in nineteenth-century Bengal of a writer making
such an abrupt shift of linguistic gear. Michael Madhusudan
Dutt, fourteen years older than Bankim and a student of Henry
Derozio, had always dreamt of being an English poet. He wrote
The Captive Ladie (1849) and *Visions of the Past* (1848) in English
and, in an imagined fellowship with the great poets of England,
dedicated one of his poems to Wordsworth. In a letter to his
friend Gaurdas Basak he wrote in English: 'I am reading Tom
Moore's life of my favourite Byron—splendid book upon my
word! Oh! how should I like to see you writing my life, if
I happen to be a great poet—which I am almost sure I shall be
if I go to England.'[13] He did go to England later; yet eventually
he came to be remembered not as a poet in English but as the
most important poet in Bangla in the nineteenth century who
energized the language, introduced new poetic forms, and drew
upon the resources of the Ramayana and Mahabharata as well
as Milton and Virgil to revitalize the rhetoric of Bangla poetry.
There was no visible opposition in his case between the decision
to write in Bangla and the admiration for Western literary
practices. One of his Bangla sonnets pays homage to 'Francisco

Petrarcha, the poet of Italy' who gave him a gem to dedicate to Saraswati 'which the goddess was pleased to accept'. This easy give-and-take between the muses of different civilizations was made possible through Dutt's familiarity with not only English and Bangla but also other European languages. A much-quoted Bangla sonnet written when Dutt was living in penury at Versailles, dramatizes the moment when he realized the folly of writing in a borrowed language. The sonnet dwells on the humiliation of begging at alien doors while the treasure-chest of his mother tongue lay unopened.[14]

Bankimchandra never made any such literary statement either about his decision to write in English or about his return to his mother tongue. If he did so in personal correspondence or conversation, these have not survived. Even after he abandoned English as a medium for imaginative literature, he remained alert to the political possibilities of English as the language of national consolidation. In the first issue of *Bangadarshan*, the journal that he founded in 1872, he wrote: 'There are certain issues that do not pertain to the Bengalis alone, where the whole of India has to be addressed. Unless we use English for such discourse, how will the rest of the country understand?'[15] But elsewhere we also find him exhorting creative writers not to write only for the educated few (which writing in English evidently implied) but to address a wider range of readers. If the use of English had a distinctly elite bias that excluded the lower class, caste and rural people, it also left out the women who might have belonged to the author's own family. In a remarkable satiric sketch Bankim makes fun of the English-knowing Bengali babu who is contemptuous of books in his mother tongue, taking pride in his familiarity with English literature. In contrast, his wife emerges as a more authentic and integrated person, who—uncontaminated by the enslaving language—enjoys Bangla fiction enthusiastically and without embarrassment. Bankim reminded his fellow writers in Bengal of this large and vital readership.

By the 1870s Bankimchandra was convinced that English was the language of polemics in India, but not of creative literature. It is well known how he admonished Romesh Chandra Dutt, a member of the heaven-born Indian Civil Service and the future author of *The Economic History of India*, for not writing in his mother tongue. In the highly westernized Dutt family to which Romesh Chandra belonged, as did his celebrated poet-cousins Toru and Oru—Bangla had never been considered a language worthy of cultivation, and he confessed a lack of formal knowledge of the language. Bankim dismissed this reason for not writing in his mother tongue, insisting that whatever educated young men like him wrote, would become the standard language. He said, 'You will never live by your writing in English . . . Look at others. Your uncles Govind Chandra and Sashi Chandra and Madhusudan Dutt were the best educated men of Hindu College in their day. Govind Chandra and Sashi Chandra's English poems will never live, Madhusudan's Bengali poetry will live as long as the Bengali language will live.'[16] These words must have created an impression on the young ICS officer, because two years later Romesh Chandra wrote his first novel *Banga-Bijeta* in 1874, and went on to write four more that have secured him a permanent place in the history of the Bangla novel.

Bankim's advice to Romesh Chandra Dutt was prophetic indeed. Except for the researcher in nineteenth-century Indian-English poetry, no one now knows the names of Sashi Chandra or Govind Chandra Dutt, nor would we have known the name of Bankimchandra Chattopadhyay if he had stopped after writing *Rajmohan's Wife*. Bankim's contemporaries may or may not have paid much attention to this novel. But reading it today, with the advantages of hindsight, we see this text as a potent site for discussing crucial questions about language, culture, colonization and representation.

Notes

THE DRAWERS OF WATER

1. In Bangla literature, as well as in songs, women carrying water in pitchers are imbued with certain romantic associations. At the time the novel was written it was a common feature of rural life, and even today in villages without piped water it remains a necessity for survival. For women this was one social occasion in the day to get out of the house, meet other women and exchange news.

2. In Bengal this month is counted from the middle of March to the middle of April.

3. This is neither a Bangla nor an English word. The author may have assumed that the reader in English would be more familiar with this broadly Orientalist word than *antahpur*. 'Zenana' also appears in the title of Chapter 5. The more commonly used Bangla word *andarmahal* is used later on p. 76.

4. Obviously the author means leafy vegetables. Salad forms no part of traditional Bengali food. This is the first of the many instances in the text where through diction an attempt has been made to confer an Englishness to Bengali experience for the benefit of an implied reader whose identity is difficult to construct because of the contradictory signs embedded in the text.

5. Detailed description of female beauty was part of the conventions of Sanskrit *kavya* literature. Since the description covered every feature from the top of the head to the toenails it was called *nakha-shikha varnan*. Bankim's subsequent Bangla novels owe much more to Sanskrit literary tradition, but even here the gravitational pull of the older models sometimes becomes evident despite his reading of British novels acting as the immediate stimulus.

6. The tributary of the Ganga that flows near Calcutta.

7. Stone collected from the Gandak river that serves as a symbol of Vishnu. The sentence is a translation of a Bengla proverb. The proverb suggests that in certain circumstances even the impossible is allowed to happen.

8. Husband's sister.

9. Kulins were supposedly very high-caste Brahmans whose males were in such demand in the marriage market that in nineteenth-century Bengal a Kulin Brahman could make a profession out of polygamy and not stay with any one wife for too long. Kanak is evidently the wife of such an absent husband.

10. The author is probably conflating the Anglo-Indian usage 'hang you' with a version of a playful Bangla abuse, literally 'Die, burnt face' (*Mor, porar-mukhi*).

THE TWO COUSINS

1. The people of West Bengal believed that they were more sophisticated and refined than those of East Bengal. The author belonged to West Bengal. One reason for this sense of superiority may have been that the colonial capital, Calcutta, and its vicinities had more luxurious buildings and gardens than agrarian East Bengal.

2. The clothes of the two men are intended to accentuate their differences in taste and temperament: one is ostentatious and the other restrained.

THE TRUANT'S RETURN HOME

1. This reference to the destroyed Biblical city—however inappropriate in the mouth of a Bengali village girl—may have been intended by the author as a phrase of friendly remonstrance, raising our curiosity about the implied reader.

2. Fish market in London. Associated with low and vituperative language. Another instance of the inscription of Englishness through diction.

THE HISTORY OF THE RISE AND PROGRESS OF A ZEMINDAR FAMILY

1. Under Hindu law, including the Dayabhaga code which was followed in Bengal, a widow was only a life-estate owner of her husband's property.

2. Legal word for widow.

3. The portions bracketed were found partly or wholly moth-eaten, and the readings have been restored by me.—B.N.B.

4. Domestic servant to the estate manager.

5. The suspicion of irony in this unusual collocation is alleviated when we find that Bankim's own Bengali version does not mention either green or old.

6. Why not 'wives in our country'? The question of the implied reader comes up here again.

A LETTER—A VISIT TO THE ZENANA

1. *Zaruri* (urgent), *wasilut* (with cost), *Sadar Amin* (district officer), *vakalatnama* (power of attorney)—all these words are from Urdu or Persian, commonly used in the legal discourse of Bengal.

2. Madhav is embroiled in many legal suits, it seems almost against his will. Apparently a landlord's duties included being involved in litigation with his neighbours.

3. For the curved knife with a floor stand used for cutting vegetables and fish, the spelling bonti would be closer to the sound.

4. Anklet.

5. A children's game played while sitting in a circle and reciting a nonsense rhyme that begins with these words.

6. Note the representation of the women's domain as a site of chaos and cacophony until the male presence brings silence and order. The aunt benevolently proclaims that 'it is woman's nature to be screaming'.

7. Father's younger brother's wife.

LOVE CAN CONQUER FEAR

1. From this chapter onwards the author intermittently steps in to make prefatory comments of an anticipatory nature, in the manner of Henry Fielding in *Tom Jones* or *Joseph Andrews*.

2. As it appears in the original.

3. Subsequently it becomes 'mango grove'.

4. The Bangla word for this tree is *bawt*, and the English synonym is banyan. As earlier in the case of zenana, the author prefers to use the Hindustani word.

5. As it appears in the original.

6. An evil spirit.

7. Feminine form of Thakur (master).

FOREWARNED AND FOREARMED

1. It is inexplicable why the servant Karuna should suddenly shriek out the abbreviated first name of the mistress when normally she never used her name.
2. As it appears in the original.
3. As it appears in the original.
4. Unit of measuring time. Roughly 24 minutes.
5. As it appears in the original.
6. In modern orthography the word is spelt *lathi*, and the wielder of a lathi would be *lathial*.
7. As it appears in the original.

WE MEET TO PART

1. So far the reader has not been given any hint about a special relationship between Madhav and Matangini.
2. Matangini's turbulent passion, concealed till now, is allowed to come to the surface. Whether or not such a speech could be articulated by a woman in the kind of culture and environment depicted so far, the generic identity of the narrative seems predicated upon this relationship. Mere husbandly oppression or wifely forbearance would not make a novel. The English models available to Bankim were all leavened with the yeast of romantic love. In this chapter, finally a man and a woman have been brought together in the context of desire. But Matangini is also made to appear sinful; thus, while becoming the heroine of a novel, she simultaneously becomes the carnal scapegoat for the *bhadralok*'s fear of the flesh.

THE RETURN

1. Shakespearean diction, presumably used to heighten the dramatic impact of the Othello-like speech.
2. The climax of the passion of love described in the previous chapter is followed here by the passion of jealousy. Both have literary antecedents.
3. Matangini is obviously not lifeless, because we see her in action in the next chapter. Perhaps the word 'about' here means 'almost'.
4. Window shutter.

WHEN THIEVES FALL OUT

1. Literal translation of a Bangla proverb. The proverb refers to the ease with which a child can be cheated.

THE FRIENDS AND THE STRANGER

1. Oh, my mother!
2. Name of the pond: *phul* = flower, *pukur* = pond.
3. Kanak refers to Rajmohan as Raju-da. The short form of his name as well as the 'da' suffix denote sisterly familiarity on her part.
4. Translation of a Bangla idiom. Literal translation of the idiom will be 'make sure that he works for it'.
5. This is an odd expression. The closest Bangla proverb denoting entreaty would translate as 'Eat my head if you do'.

THE PROTECTRESS

1. Mathur Ghose's large and unkempt house is described in such detail partly because the conventions of realism as learnt from the English novels demanded specificity of observation, and partly because the mysterious set of rooms in the godown, which form part of the plot later, had to be explained. The shabbiness of the house is also intended to indicate Mathur's unrefined ways.
2. References to Angelo or Guido may be in deference to the cultured frame of reference of the English-educated reader.
3. As it appears in the original.
4. In some other places the same variety of trees are referred to as areca nut.
5. Back entrance of a house.
6. The simile comparing ten-armed Durga with a crab sounds rather unorthodox.
7. Bankim is probably making some kind of cultural point here about the dissemination of European influence by insisting that, even in the house of a non-westernized rural family in Bengal, a picture of the Virgin and Child hangs on the wall along with those of Durga and Kali.
8. It is difficult to see what other complexion a young Indian woman could have. The word brunette comes from books of fiction rather than from first-hand usage in life.
9. The external, male part of a household, as opposed to andarmahal.

BETWEEN RIVAL CHARMERS

1. Hair braided and piled up in a knot or a chignon.
2. Another example of East Bengal–West Bengal rivalry, now in terms of the elegance and propriety of women's hairstyles.
3. As it appears in the original.
4. A small box.
5. As it appears in the original.

THE VIGILANCE OF LOVE

1. Urdu words commonly used in Bangla.

CAPTORS AND CAPTIVE

1. Literally 'bureaucrat', here it means a subordinate officer.

MADHAV AND TARA

1. The importance of childhood friendship in the novels of this period is significant because that was the only time boys and girls could meet freely. Bankim's novel *Chandrashekhar* (1875) dealt with a childhood love that was thwarted by an arranged marriage. In this chapter, however, the author attempts to de-eroticize the relationship by an explicit statement at the end of the paragraph.
2. This emphasizes the equality in their relationship. Normally, Tara, being the older, would be addressed as *didi*.
3. Husband's younger brother.
4. This gratuitous explanation of female gullibility may have been prompted by the fact that in this novel the women are actually much stronger and more courageous than the men.
5. This splendour of decor seems unexpected in Mathur's crude dungeon, but the gorgeous setting and the pale beauty on the mahogany bed—still unravished, though emaciated through starvation—reiterate motifs of late eighteenth-century Gothic fiction in Britain.

THE LAST CHAPTER IN LIFE'S BOOK—AND IN THIS

1. Directly reminiscent of Thackeray's authorial dialogue with the reader, it may also be read as a deliberate evocation of the conventions of oral narrative.

2. As it appears in the original.

3. Bankimchandra had already been a Deputy Magistrate for six years when he wrote this novel and had had direct experience of the way the police functioned.

4. It should be noted that the bringer of justice is an Irishman and not a British officer.

CONCLUSION

1. Tying up the threads of a story neatly at the end and meting out just rewards was a convention of Victorian fiction, as seen in the last chapters of the novels of Dickens, Thackeray or George Eliot.

AFTERWORD

1. Some of them are: Sisir Kumar Das (*The Artist in Chains: The Life of Bankimchandra Chatterjee*, New Delhi, 1984); Tapan Raychaudhuri (*Europe Reconsidered: Perceptions of the West in Nineteenth-Century Bengal*, Delhi, 1988); Jasodhara Bagchi ('Positivism and Nationalism: Womanhood and Crisis in Nationalist Fiction: Bankimchandra's *Anandamath*', in *Narrative: Forms and Transformations*, eds Sudhakar Marathe and Meenakshi Mukherjee, Delhi, 1986); Sabyasachi Bhattacharya (in *Bankimchandra: Essays in Perspective*, ed. Bhabatosh Chatterjee, Calcutta: Sahitya Akademi, 1994); Ranajit Guha (*Indian Historiography of India: A Nineteenth-Century Agenda*, Calcutta, 1985); Tanika Sarkar (*Bankimchandra and the Impossibility of a Political Agenda*, New Delhi: Occasional Papers Series of NMML, 1991); Partha Chatterjee (*Nationalist Thought and the Colonial World*, New Delhi, 1986); and Sudipta Kaviraj (*The Unhappy Consciousness: Bankimchandra Chattopadhyay and the Formation of Nationalist Consciousness in India*, Delhi, 1995).

2. Nirad C. Chaudhuri wrote: 'The two men who created modern Bengali literature wrote their first works in English before they even thought of writing anything in Bengali. The creator of modern Bengali poetry wrote his first long poem in English, and the creator of Bengali fiction his first novel. But both of them found that to do so was to go into a blind alley which led nowhere. For this reason they turned to Bengali . . .' ('Opening Address', *The Eye of the Beholder*, ed. Maggie Butcher, London, 1983).

Sisir Kumar Das wrote: '[*Rajmohan's Wife*] was little known outside an intimate circle and was soon forgotten . . . Bankim thought of translating this into Bengali, and in fact he did translate the first nine chapters. He did not complete the job perhaps because he thought it was too unsatisfactory to receive any public attention' (*The Artist in Chains: The Life of Bankimchandra Chatterjee*, New Delhi, 1984, p. 19).

Jogesh Chandra Bagal wrote: 'Bankim's literary temperament could not be satisfied with writing fiction in English and . . . he began writing *Durgeshnandini*' (my translation) (*Bankim Rachanabali*, vol. 1, Calcutta: Sahitya Samsad, first pub. 1955, present edn 1980, p. xiv).

3. 'Bankim Chandra Chatterjee by a Bengali', *Induprakash*, 16 July to 27 August 1894. These articles were signed 'Zero'. The present quotation is from the fifth article, 'His Literary History', reprinted in *The Harmony of Virtue*, p. 90.

4. Two very characteristic statements included in this volume, *Bankimchandra: Essays in Perspective* (ed. Bhabatosh Chatterjee, Calcutta: Sahitya Akademi, 1994), are quoted below:

'Bankim started his literary journey with *Rajmohan's Wife* written in English, but his real achievement began with *Durgeshnandini*' (Saroj Bandopadhyay, p. 449).

'*Rajmohan's Wife* shows no sign of genius, nor did it arouse much interest among the readers when it was being serialized. This literary effort by India's first Bachelor of Arts—Bankimchandra—was in the same mould as all the other poems, stories and essays that used to be written in those days by those who had newly been educated in English' (Sunil Gangopadhyay, p. 390).

There is, however, one critic in this volume who does not dismiss this novel, but her claim that the novel had 'immediate readership' all over India is not substantiated by evidence: 'Because it [*Rajmohan's Wife*] transcended the linguistic barrier, the novel gained immediate readership from Indians who belonged to states other than Bengal' (Prema Nandkumar, p. 400).

The tendency to claim Bankimchandra as an originary figure of the Indian novel in English is a very recent one. Ganeshwar Mishra elsewhere writes: '[Bankim] considerably influenced the Indo-Anglian and Indian language writers of the late nineteenth and early twentieth century' ('The Indian Narrative Tradition and Bankim Chandra's

Rajmohan's Wife', *Journal of Literary Studies*, vol. 4, no. 1, p. 59). While Bankim certainly influenced Indian-language writers—not only in Bangla but, through a chain of translations, some writers in Hindi, Marathi and Kannada as well—the claim that he influenced Indian writers in English would be very hard to sustain, even though he may be the unwitting founder of a genre that now has high visibility.

5. For a detailed description of the emergence of the novel in Indian languages, see chapters I and II of Meenakshi Mukherjee, *Realism and Reality: The Novel and Society in India*, Delhi, 1985.

6. See 'The Burden of English Studies', Gayatri Chakraborty Spivak, in *The Lie of the Land: English Literary Studies in India*, ed. Rajeshwari Sunder Rajan, Delhi, 1992.

7. See Chapter IV, 'Women in a New Genre', in *Realism and Reality*.

8. Quoted by Sudhir Chandra in *The Oppressive Present: Literature and Social Consciousness in Colonial India*, Delhi, 1992, p. 8.

9. From the English translation of Rabindranath Tagore's *Jibansmriti* (Bangla, 1912) published as *My Reminiscences*, New York, 1914, p. 181.

10. 'Opening Address' by Nirad C. Chaudhuri in *The Eye of the Beholder*, ed. Maggie Butcher, London, 1983, p. 11.

11. See Introduction of *Madhusudan Rachanabali*, ed. Kshetra Gupta, Calcutta: Sahitya Samsad, 1965.

12. Nirad C. Chaudhuri in *The Eye of the Beholder*, p. 10.

13. See p. xiii, *Madhusudan Rachanabali*.

14. Sonnet 3 in 'Chaturdashpadi Kavitavali', p. 159, *Madhusudan Rachanabali*.

15. Quoted by the editor, Jogesh Chandra Bagal, in *Bankim Rachanabali*, vol. 1, Calcutta: Sahitya Samsad, 1955, p. xvi.

16. Quoted by the editor, Jogesh Chandra Bagal, in *Romesh Rachanabali*, Calcutta: Sahitya Samsad, 1960, p. xxvii.